Life
DEATH &
GOLD
LEATHER
trousers

ABOUT THE AUTHOR

Fiona Foden grew up in a tiny Yorkshire village called Goose Eye. At seventeen, she landed her dream job on a teenage magazine in Scotland, and went on to be editor of *Bliss*, *More!* and *Just Seventeen* magazines. For two years she lived on a narrowboat in London, but moved back on to dry land when her twin sons, Sam and Dexter, and daughter, Erin, were born. She and her husband, Jimmy, also have a rescue dog called Jack.

Although Fiona has written five novels for adults, this is her first book for children. Apart from writing, which she does every single day, Fiona also loves to draw, run, cook, play her saxophone, ride her bike, sit making notes in cafés and soak in a bubble bath. She lives with her family in Scotland.

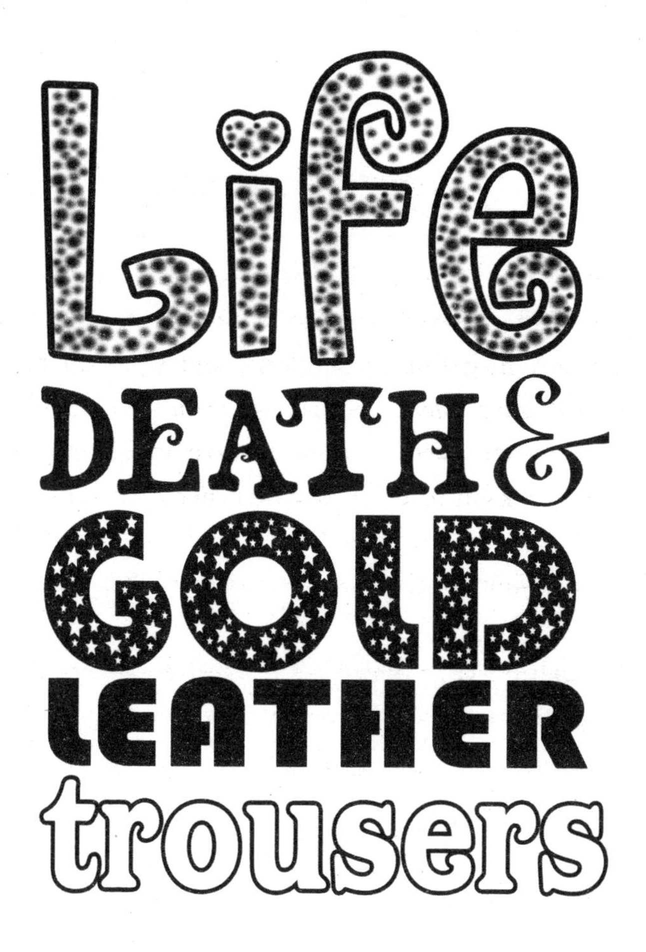

Fiona Foden

SCHOLASTIC

First published in the UK in 2011 by Scholastic Children's Books
An imprint of Scholastic Ltd
Euston House, 24 Eversholt Street
London, NW1 1DB, UK
Registered office: Westfield Road, Southam, Warwickshire, CV47 0RA

ISBN 978 1407 12086 7

A CIP catalogue record for this book is available
from the British Library.

Printed by CPI Bookmarque, Croydon CR0 4TD
Papers used by Scholastic Children's Books are made
from wood grown in sustainable forests.

1 3 5 7 9 10 8 6 4 2

www.scholastic.co.uk/zone

For Sam, Dex and Erin with love

27 Ocean Road
Copper Beach
Devon
EX11 7FK

14 June

Dear Jupe,
Yes, I know. This is weird because you're dead. But hear me out for a minute, OK? It's me – Clover. Remember me? Yeah, of course you do. In fact, I've written you tons of letters over the years, which seems a bit old-fashioned – I mean, no one writes real letters, do they, with pens and envelopes and everything? And you never wrote back – not once, even after I'd gone to the trouble of stealing stamps out of the kitchen drawer! Anyway, I still liked writing. It felt a bit like talking to you and that's something I haven't been able to do in a very long time. And now I won't be able to ever again.

I could hardly believe it when Mum came into my room this morning and sat down on the edge of my bed. She was all nervous, twisting her hands together, so I knew it was something bad. "Um, Clover?" she said in a small voice. "Remember

Uncle Jupe?" I nodded and felt my chest go tight. "He's . . . he's passed away, love," she explained, clearing her throat. I just nodded and willed myself not to cry. We'd all spent a long time pretending you no longer existed so I had to pretend I was OK.

So I just asked why you died.

Mum's face crumpled a bit, then she said, "He had cancer. If only we'd known. . ." Then she jumped up from my bed and rushed out of my room. I was glad about that. In front of Mum, I had to pretend to be normal about you dying when actually I remember every tiniest thing about you, even though I haven't seen you since I was ten. I know you stopped sending birthday cards. No hard feelings, OK? But just to update you, I am thirteen next Friday. I make that three birthdays owing!

I remember coming to your funny, crumbly house in Cornwall where Fuzz was always prowling about. You used to feed him fresh salmon and spoil him rotten. And he'd hiss and spit at me. You said he thought I was a rival cat with my narrow green eyes and wild black hair that looked just like his fur. Thanks, Jupe! Even back then, I didn't want to look like I had a fuzzy cat plonked on my head.

I forgave you, though. For as long as I can remember, I wanted to be a real musician like you when you were young. I wanted to travel the world and play for thousands of fans. I wasn't so sure about the mad curly hair or the tight leather trousers (GOLD leather trousers, ahem!) or your frilly pink women's blouses. But I could imagine it all – the music and screaming all rolled into one massive noise. It made my heart beat faster just thinking about it.

By the time I was born you weren't a pop star any more, so this is hard to believe – but Mum said fans used to throw knickers at you. I wouldn't fancy being pelted with other people's stinky old pants, but I still caught it. No – not the knickers. The music thing, I mean. You'd sit me down with all your different guitars and make the chord shapes while I strummed, so it sounded like it was me playing. Then, when I got a bit better and my fingers were stronger, it really WAS me.

You changed my life, Jupe. You taught me to play and we'd sit for hours, strumming together like it was our own little world. You treated me like your friend, not a kid, and even though Mum and my teachers get annoyed with me sometimes, you never did. So I always felt good being around you. Not like I was going to mess up or look stupid.

Now you're gone. At school they're always lecturing us about drugs and smoking and alcohol. But no one ever talks about death.

I wish I could undo the terrible thing I did that made us all fall out, Jupe. It was my fault and I'm sorry. Even more than that, I'm sorry you died.

To make up for everything, the only thing I can

think of is to be the best guitarist I can possibly be and form a real band and be amazing. What d'you think? I'm going to do it – that's an actual promise. So listen out for me, even when it gets really rowdy up there with all those angels strumming their harps.

Love,
Clover xxx

P.S. I'm not posting this letter, obviously. I just wanted to talk to you like I used to when it felt like I could say whatever popped into my head. Anyway, dead people can't read (I don't think).

1

Birthday Bombshell

Thirteen's too young for a midlife crisis, don't you agree? It's supposed to happen when you're old and start shrieking, "The grass needs cutting, hasn't anyone noticed? Are we going for a jungle effect out there? Shall we throw in a few baboons while we're at it?" That's the kind of thing Mum says. She grabs an idea and runs away with it like an out-of-control horse. As for me, Clover Jones – well, despite being supposedly in the *best years of my life* (snort), my brain's gone into meltdown.

It starts with shouting downstairs – Mum and Dad barking at each other like dogs. *Yap yap yap!* (Mum: small, persistent dog. The kind that snaffles around your ankles, looking like it'll widdle at any moment.) *Woof woof woof!* (Dad: large hound with thunderous growl, but soft and lovable really.) At first, when I wake up, I actually assume real dogs are fighting outside. Then Mum yells something clearly. I know some dogs are super-intelligent, but I've never heard of one that can shout, "I can't believe what you're telling me, Geoffrey!"

Then I know it's not dogs, but humans. More accurately, my parents, having one humongous row. Hello Shame Street (this leads to Embarrassment Central).

Embarrassment Central is where you wind up when your parents fight in earshot of your best friend. You see, it's not just me in my bedroom. My little sister Lily's away on a sleepover, so Mum said I could have Jess to stay last night. Using only my eye muscles, I swivel my gaze towards her. My best friend is lying on her side in Lily's bed with her mouth open. She's either *really* asleep, or trying to protect me from maximum humiliation by breathing slow and deep, like a real sleeping person.

I suspect the latter. If Jupe wasn't dead, even *he'd* be able to hear Mum and Dad a three-hour drive away in Cornwall. In fact, maybe he still can from his cloud.

I creep out of bed and pad downstairs in my birthday pyjamas. What I plan to say is, "Mum, Dad, Jess is here – remember?" Because they've probably forgotten.

I tiptoe towards the kitchen, starting to feel a little less brave. They're muttering now, and I start wishing we could rewind to yesterday when I became a teenager at last. That was an embarrassing day too. But at least it only involved Betty next door cooing, "Ooh, Clover, you're a teenager! And I remember you wetting your dungarees in Superdrug when you were little. One of the girls had to fetch a mop and bucket!" It's not exactly the kind of thing you want to be reminded of, but a bit of wee in Superdrug is nothing compared to this.

Now I'm peeping round the kitchen door. Dad's standing in front of our fridge with his hands pressed against it. "Just . . . go," Mum spits out, not realizing I'm here. At least I don't *think* she's realized. I can't see her face, only the back of her, with her burgundy hair crinkling down her back, mussed up like a bush. She's wearing her shiny black nightie and pink satin slippers. One nightie strap dangles from her bony shoulder.

I can't run back upstairs, because they'll hear me and think I've been spying and get mad. I can't bring myself to march into the kitchen either. Dad backs further against the fridge. He looks like he wants to disappear right inside it, along with our murky yoghurts and antique cheese. Some of the things in there are older than Lily. Behind Dad are our fridge poetry magnets – words you can arrange to make surreal sentences like ABNORMAL BANGLES BURN TEAPOT. The phrase YOUR FURRY EYEBALL hovers above Dad's left shoulder.

Dad spots me and frowns. "Clover, sweetheart," he croaks, "could you leave us alone for a moment, please?"

"It's just, um, Jess is upstairs—" I begin.

"No," Mum announces, swinging round to face me. "Clover deserves to know what's going on. Why don't *you* tell her, Geoffrey?"

My breath catches in my throat.

"I'm sorry, Clover," Dad murmurs, looking down at his old brown slippers. It's then that I register the tartan zip-up bag at his feet. Thoughts zap through my brain: he's going to work away from home, like Mia Burnett's dad, who does something with minerals in Peru. Or maybe he's just going to normal work. But he's not wearing his overalls – and anyway, it's Saturday. Dad's a garage mechanic and usually has weekends off. And why would he take a tartan bag to the garage?

Then, before I can convince myself everything's going to be OK, and he really *is* only going to work, he picks up the bag and marches right past me. Street noises waft in as he opens the front door; then there's a bang as he shuts it.

Dad's gone. In his old brown slippers.

I stare at Mum. "What's happening?" I whisper.

She looks at me. I know it sounds mad, but I'm transfixed by her face. On a normal morning she'd have full make-up on by now. She'd have the pink blusher, the smoky grey eyeshadow, the burgundy lipstick and layer upon layer of Lavish Lash black mascara. Today is obviously not a Lavish Lash kind of day. "You . . . you know Dad's life drawing class?" she says faintly.

"Uh-huh. . ." I once had a peek at Dad's drawings. I wished on our hamster's life that I hadn't. Mum and Dad aren't the types to stroll about in the nude, and I'd never realized how lumpy and hairy and kind of collapsed-looking adults' bodies can be. If you looked like that, wouldn't you keep your clothes *on*, at least in public? I mean, why would you let people draw you?

"He's . . . he's met some woman there," Mum says.

Something crashes inside me, as if I've been punched hard in the belly. "What d'you mean?" I blurt out.

"Just that, love. He's met . . . a woman." She wipes her fingers across her sore-looking eyes. "I don't know how else to explain it."

"But, Mum. . ."

"Clover, look, I'm so sorry. . ."

"He's coming back, though, isn't he?" I cry. "I mean, he's not . . . he's not gone for *good*, has he?"

Mum nods and her eyes are all shiny again. "He wants to be with her. That's what he said. . ."

"But he can't!" I yell. "He lives here, with us!" It's now starting to feel like a really sick joke. My dad, meeting another woman? But he's old! And he's a father. What about me, Lily and Mum? I glance towards the kitchen doorway, willing Jess not to come downstairs all smiley and normal. I want her to sleep for a hundred years, like the princess who ate the poisoned apple.

"He used to," Mum declares, looking angry now instead of sad. "Your father *used* to live with us, Clover. Not any more."

With that, she flops on to a kitchen chair and stares ahead like a ghost. I stand there, opening and shutting my mouth like some kind of demented fish. I know I should do something more useful, like hug Mum and say everything'll be all right. But all I can do is stand here, being a fish.

There's the creak of a bedroom door, followed by soft footsteps on the landing. "*Clover!*" Jess sing-songs from upstairs. "What are you doing?"

"Just a minute!" I yell up – but too late. Jess bounds downstairs and into the kitchen in her polka-dot nightie. Her long, light brown hair's tied back, and her cheeks are pink and shiny. She looks like an advert for healthy living. "Um, OK if I have a drink?" she asks, glancing from me to Mum.

"Course it is," I say, diving to the fridge for orange juice.

"Well, girls," Mum announces, "help yourself to anything you like. I'm not feeling too good, so I'm going back to bed for a little nap, all right?" She scurries away in a flurry of black satin nightie.

I hand Jess a glass of juice. "What's happened?" she whispers.

"I, um. . ." I begin. I sort of want to tell her. But it's so huge, I don't know where to start. "It's Dad," I mutter. A squeak from the back porch makes me flinch. Cedric, our hamster, is running like blazes on his wheel. Why can't I have the simple, monotonous life of a hamster?

"Probably just a silly argument over nothing," Jess says, touching my arm. "My parents yell at each other all the time."

No, they don't. They call each other "angel" and "sweetcakes" and are always patting and stroking each other. "No, it's more than that," I insist. "Dad's. . ." I want to say "left us" but it clogs in my throat. "He's gone," I add lamely.

"God, Clover. Are you sure?"

"Yeah. That's what Mum says. . ."

"That's awful!" she cries. "Did you have any idea?"

I shake my head.

"Want me to stick around for a while?" Jess asks. "We're supposed to be visiting Auntie Sue in Exeter, but I'll stay if you want. Mum won't mind if I don't go. . ."

"No, it's OK," I say firmly.

"Sure?"

"Honestly. Mum probably wants to talk." Actually, it's what *I* want. I don't feel like having anyone here, not even Jess. I want to grab my guitar and play and play until everything's fixed again.

Jess nods and hugs me. "Great birthday present, huh?" she says.

I try for a laugh, but all that pops out is a tiny, Cedric-sized squeak.

2

Our Nudie Model Shame

When Mum creeps out from her bedroom two hours later, I learn a few vital facts.

1. Dad hasn't gone off with one of the students, but a *model.* "One of those women who drape themselves over a chair or whatever, stark naked," Mum snarls, banging the teapot on to the worktop. I can't believe it. All I can picture is Dad walking arm-in-arm with a terrible pencil drawing, and not a real woman at all.
2. This has, according to Mum, been going on for months.
3. The thought of Dad doing anything with anybody is almost enough to make me run out and spew in the garden. The only thing that stops me is the thought of Betty peering over the fence and watching me. *Strange girl, that Clover. Peed in Superdrug, was sick on her lawn . . . now what other embarrassing things might she do?*

The front door flies open. "I'm back!" Lily yells, clattering into the kitchen and flinging her sleepover bag on to the table.

"Hey," I say, trying to normalize my voice. "How was it?"

"Awesome," she enthuses. "Why are you wearing your nightie, Mum?"

"Oh, guess I forgot to get dressed," Mum says with a small laugh. I glance at the kitchen clock. It's twelve-thirty. Will she ever wear proper daytime clothes again, or drift around in her nightie to parents' evenings, school concerts, everything? There's a woman down the road who comes out in a grey bra and jogging bottoms held up with a dressing gown cord. Will Mum turn into *that?*

"Are you sick?" Lily asks with a frown.

"No, I'm not sick," Mum says wearily. "I'm just a bit . . . tired, that's all. Where's Hannah? Did her mum just drop you off?"

"Yeah, 'cause they're in a rush for the swimming gala."

Swimming galas. Trips to Auntie Sue's. Other people's lives are so cosy and normal. "Right." Mum looks relieved. A tense pause fills the kitchen, and I don't know what to do. The inside of my mouth feels sawdusty, like the bottom of Cedric's cage. Is it my job to tell Lily about Dad and the nudie model? I only turned thirteen yesterday. I don't feel ready for the responsibility. Mum sips tea from her chipped World's Best Mum mug.

"Where's Dad?" Lily asks.

My heart staggers in my chest. *Tell her, Mum. Tell her.*

Mum sips some more.

"I said where's—"

"He's . . . not here," I cut in. "He's . . . gone away."

Mum seems to draw herself up then, as if her tea has magical, strength-giving powers. "Lily, sweetheart. Me and Daddy . . . we're . . . he's . . . gone-to-live-somewhere-else."

Lily's mouth wilts. "What? Where's he gone?"

I go over and squeeze her hand, noticing that each of her stubby nails has been painted a different colour. Her shoulder-length dark hair hangs messily around her face.

"We're not sure yet," Mum says softly, "but whatever happens, we'll be fine, OK? Everything will work out. Won't it, Clover?"

How the heck should I know? "Suppose so," I mumble.

Lily inhales deeply. I can tell she's trying to flatten the wobble in her voice as she announces, "Guess what! Hannah's got a chocolate fountain."

And that, in a nutshell, is how my little sister's mind works. It flits on to something else – something less scary than nudie models, like chocolate fountains or wanting to buy a plastic tunnel to stop Cedric keeling over from boredom on his wheel.

★

I'm worried about Mum, but I don't know what to *do* with her. Every time I try to cuddle her or offer her more tea, she shrugs me off as if she doesn't want to be cuddled. "I'm swimming in tea!" she wails at one point. What else could I offer her? Wine? No – I can imagine how that'd end up. So I pack our swimming stuff and set off with Lily into town, which feels better than being trapped in our house.

I'll figure out what to do when we get back. In fact, by that time, Dad'll have realized that he can't live another second without us and come rushing home, and I'll pretend that my demented brain just made the whole episode up.

3

Operation Normal

As we walk into town, Lily fires questions about Dad. I can't answer a single one. Then she gives up and starts telling me all these scintillating facts about Hannah's chocolate fountain. Like how Hannah's mum adds oily stuff to stop the chocolate setting rock solid. How dipped strawberries are good, but marshmallows are a bit sickly, so Lily could only manage about thirty-seven.

By the time we reach town, I'm all chocolated out.

Normally, on a sunny Saturday like this, we'd head straight for the North Cove. Our town, Copper Beach, is named after its weird rust-coloured sand. Loads of people used to come here for their holidays. You can see from old photos that the hotels along the seafront used to be mad, clashing colours, like Jupe in his gold leather trousers and women's blouses. You'd get pink, yellow and turquoise buildings all next to one another. Then people stopped coming and the hotels faded and their paint peeled off. Everyone wanted to go to Ibiza or

Disneyland. I've never been abroad but imagine a sky so blue it hurts your eyes, and sea as warm as a bath.

Lily and I head down the stone steps to the North Cove. "Don't feel like swimming," she announces.

I stop. "Me neither, Lil. Where shall we go?"

She grins, showing the gap that the tooth fairy didn't pay for because she forgot. "The pet shop. Please, Clover! You promised we'd buy Cedric that tunnel."

I sigh. "OK." We head for the shops and she pulls me into Pet Heaven, where we watch the tiny neon fish fluttering like sweet wrappers in their tanks. "What are they thinking about?" Lily muses.

"Not much," I say. "They're only meant to have three-second memories."

"They must think about *something*," she insists.

"Yeah, well, they're probably thinking, What a fantastic new tank! Imagine if your home looked completely new and different every three seconds."

The phrase "broken home" pops into my head, and I picture our house cracking down the middle with our favourite possessions – my guitar, Lily's giant tub of five hundred felt tips – poking out of the rubble. I want to forget this morning, to erase it like one of Dad's horrible drawings. I want a three-second memory, like a fish.

"Look – kittens!" Lily exclaims, swooping towards a wire cage at the back of the shop. "Can we buy one?"

"No way. Mum's allergic to cats, remember?"

"Well. . ." She frowns, and I can virtually hear her

brain whirring. "We could get one for Betty. She's looked awfully lonely since Midnight was run over."

"But what if she doesn't want a new one?" I reason. "You can't replace people's pets without asking them." Unlike people, obviously. We're *completely* replaceable.

"Stinking meanie," Lily says with a sniff.

"Because I won't buy a kitten? Don't be so stupid!"

Lily chews her lip. "Let's get Cedric's tunnel then. Did you bring your birthday money?"

"Oh, right, I thought I was a *stinking meanie. . .*"

She juts out her lip. "Sorry."

"Oh, OK," I say, sighing. Now the Dad thing's happened, I can't think of anything I want to buy anyway. The tunnel is made from amber plastic, and I have to agree that Cedric will love its twists and turns. "Where shall we go now?" Lily asks outside the shop.

I rack my brain. The last thing I want is to go shopping in the precinct. On Saturdays you're always bound to run into someone like Sophie Skelling, who's already got 34C boobs, trying on a teeny custard-yellow crochet bikini in New Look. My own swimsuit's plain navy blue. "It's not plain," Mum insisted when she bought it for me. "It's *sporty*."

"Let's just go home," I say, "and give Cedric his present."

We don't talk much on the way back. I think Lily's feeling as sad and hollow as I am. As we walk, I decide to embark on "Operation Normal" and make a list in my head of ordinary things to reassure me that life will carry on and be fine.

<u>Some Normal Things</u>
Swimming galas
Visits to aunties
Chocolate fountains
Cedric
Dad pottering about the greenhouse. . .

No – not Dad! Anything but Dad. I try to think of more things but my mind's a blank. And I don't feel any better.

Back home, Mum's lying on the sofa with her bare feet up against the wall, babbling away on the phone. Spotting us, she finishes the call and smiles weakly. "Have a nice time in town, girls?"

"Yeah," Lily says. "Look what we bought Cedric. . ."

Mum blinks at the tunnel as if she hasn't the faintest idea what it's for. "It's for him to run in," I explain. "To stop him getting bored in his cage."

"Oh!" Mum says with a forced smile. "That's nice, love. He'll like that."

"Let's show him," Lily says, tugging me out to our back porch, where Cedric lives. We call it a porch, but it's really a wobbly outbuilding that Dad built with planks he found in skips. I have a trick that always makes everyone laugh, and decide to perform it to cheer up Mum. I lift Cedric from his cage and let him pat-pat on my hand. Then I carry him through to the living room to show her. "Watch this," I say. Mum watches with red-rimmed eyes. Then, right on cue, Cedric scampers up the sleeve of my top, around the back of my neck with a delicious tickle and down the other sleeve, where he pings out to rapturous applause.

OK, so Mum doesn't clap exactly. And I feel so stupid as I shuffle out to the porch to put Cedric back in his cage. I might come up with some mad ideas sometimes, but what on earth made me think I could cheer up poor Mum with a performing rodent?

4

Beauty Tip 1 (Don't Try This at Home)

By Monday morning I've convinced myself that the whole school will be laughing its pants off about my dad running off with a naked model person. I'm fretting about this before I've even got out of bed. Lily is up already, chatting non-stop to Mum downstairs, as if trying her best to pretend that everything's normal. Poor kid. Normally she only has this kind of stuff to worry about:

1. Finding acceptable munchies in the cupboard for school snack (no cheesy Wotsits? Call Childline!).
2. And a pair of matching socks.
3. Which hair bobble she's going to wear that day.
4. Remembering her Brownie Promise and Law.

I huddle under my duvet, trying to think of more things, but can't. Which pretty much makes my point.

"Clover!" Mum shouts up. "Are you dressed yet? Or

are you planning to go to school in your pyjamas today?"

She's one to talk. She wore her nightie all of Saturday, even to answer the door when a man came around selling dusters out of a suitcase. "Sorry," I heard him say, "I shouldn't disturb you when you're ill."

I guess she is ill, in a way. She's trying to be normal, but I can tell she's putting on a cheerful act, even from up here in my bedroom. "Clover!" Mum calls up again. "It's gone eight o'clock, love. . ."

I jump out of bed, tear off my PJs and pull on my alluring grey school skirt plus polo shirt in the hideous colour they call "bronze". It's actually a pale, pukey beige which makes everyone look corpse-like, apart from Sophie Skelling with her tumbling curls and spray-on tan.

In the bathroom I drag a comb through my hair. Mum calls it "ebony", but it's actually very-dark-brown-nearly-black. It's currently sticking up lumpenly at the top, looks OK-ish for about five centimetres below that, then frizzles down to my shoulders. My big fat fringe is a disaster.

Raking among Mum's miracle potions in the bathroom cabinet, I find a bottle of golden serum stuff and dollop some on to my hair. It feels a bit greasy but hopefully it'll produce wondrous tresses à la Skelling. Maybe it'll make me 34C-bra-shaped while I'm at it, and worthy of yellow crochet bikinis. I brush my teeth, grab my bag and guitar from my room and hurry downstairs in the hope of a luscious breakfast laid out by Momma.

Only today there's not much in the way of breakfast. Lily's parked at the table, tucking into little piles of things from the same plate, like Mum used to give us for lunch when we were little. There's a raisin pile, a tinned sweetcorn pile and a small mound of grated cheese. Lily's obviously been allowed to assemble her own breakfast. It looks like some kind of weird nutritional experiment. I find the cornflakes box and shake it. Empty, apart from orangey dust at the bottom. No Sugar Puffs either. Fantastic. I peer into the bread bin, find the last two slices of a loaf and quickly make myself some toast. When I bite into it, though, I couldn't feel less like eating, and can barely gulp it down.

"You'd better hurry," Mum says, patting my shoulder.

"I'm just not hungry," I mutter. "C'mon, hurry up, Lily. Let's go."

She crams a fistful of raisins into her mouth and leaps up from her chair. We're cutting it fine time-wise. I wonder if Dad's at work yet, or will they live off Nudie's money? You must be paid loads for that kind of work. Otherwise, why would you do it? At least Mum's dressed today, and will be working later, which has to be better than sitting around moping all day. Lily and I pull on our jackets. "Have a good day, darlings," Mum calls out. We're almost out of the front door when she scampers after us. "Clover, what have you got on your hair?" she asks.

"Nothing," I say.

"It's very greasy," Mum says with a frown. "What have you put on it?"

Uh-oh. It was probably some of her skincare gloop that cost more than our TV. Even though Mum's really pretty, she's convinced she needs all these creams and oils to stop herself shrivelling into an old woman. "Some, er, stuff from the bathroom cabinet," I babble, horribly aware of the spectre of Skelling across the road. She's wearing the shortest school skirt she could possibly get away with, all the better to show off her long, tanned legs. She grins fakely and waves.

I flap my hand at her as Mum rakes through my hair as if checking for nits. "Mum, stop it, we'll be *late*," I protest. From around the corner saunters – no, please no – Riley Hart, tousle-haired and heart-stoppingly cute, doing his long-legged gangly walk. I stagger away from Mum. I *think* Riley smiles over at me. His fair fringe springs over his eyes, and his hands are thrust into his trouser pockets. Since he moved here after Christmas, Copper Beach has felt brighter, as if glitter has been sprinkled over it.

"Is it some kind of oil?" Mum asks.

"I don't know. . ."

"Come on, you must know. *You* put it on. . ."

I clear my throat. "It was that yellowy stuff in the thin bottle."

"For God's sake, Clover!" she exclaims. "That's olive oil. I thought I could smell something *salady*. . ."

"Ew, disgusting," Lily sniggers at my side.

"What was olive oil doing in the bathroom?" I snap, aware of Skelling dawdling to let Riley catch up with her as usual. Best mates, those two, always chatting away. Oh, the joys of living on the flight path to school so nearly everyone passes our house.

"It's been there for years," Mum says, "since Lily was little and I'd rub it into her scalp to get rid of the flaky bits. . ."

I try to stomp back inside, but Mum blocks the doorway. "Mum, I'll have to have a shower, wash it off. . ."

"You can't have a shower at twenty-five to nine. . ."

"I can't go to school covered in oil either!"

Mum plants her hands on her hips. "I'm sorry, but you'll have to," she says firmly. "Look on the bright side, love. Olive oil's a brilliant conditioner."

I open my mouth to protest, then turn and march schoolwards with Lily whooping like a monkey at my side. The day can only get better.

Q. What's Brown and Stinky?

My school's called Horsedung (its real name is Horsedon but no one calls it that). It's a huge brown lump, and it stinks – at least before lunch while the dinner ladies are brewing up hideous potions to pollute our insides. I know school meals are meant to be healthy, but the government's rules don't seem to have reached our little corner of Devon. We never have stuff at home to make a packed lunch, and Mum won't let me go to the chippie, which seem a little unfair as she works there and daily fried food hasn't done *her* any harm.

Once I've dropped off Lily at primary school, I leg it up the hill. I'm beyond late, which *does* seem to matter now. I also hope that if I run, the air whooshing through my hair will evaporate the olive oil.

All through registration and maths, I keep my head down, horribly conscious of the salady pong. Break time is trickier. In need of some friendly support, I grab Jess and make her come to the loos with me. Luckily, there's no one else in there. "Try washing it out," she suggests. Obediently, I rub on a splodge of pink liquid soap from the dispenser and splash some warm water on to my head. "Think it'll work?" I ask doubtfully.

"Course it will," Jess reassures me. "Soap's just like shampoo, isn't it?"

Not like Jess's shampoo, it isn't. Hers has exotic ingredients like mango essence and rare orchid juice or whatever. While Mum buys herself fancy wrinkle creams, Lily and I get cheapo shampoo that's ninety-nine pence for something like sixty-five litres. It's bright blue and smells of hospitals.

School soap, on the other hand, smells bubblegum-sweet and soon works up into a creamy froth. "Wash it off in the basin," instructs Jess. "Here, I'll help you."

I fill a basin and dunk in my humiliated head while she sloshes on water from her cupped hands. It runs down my polo shirt and swills inside my burning ears. "Is it done yet?" I ask, my voice echoing around the basin.

"No," she mutters. "The more I rinse, the more bubbly it gets. It's really frothing up now. . ."

"How will I get it off?" Panic judders up my chest.

"God, Clover, I don't know. . ."

"I can't go to history with a bubbly head!" I wail.

"Maybe we can pat it with paper towels," she says desperately.

"*Patting* won't work, it'll still be frothy. . ."

The loo door bangs open. "What's the matter, Jess?" comes Skelling's crowing voice. "Hey, Clover, is that you with your head in the sink? Didn't you have time for a shower this morning? Thought I could smell something. . ."

I flip my head out of the water like a seal. "There was some, er, stuff in my hair," I say coolly.

"What, like bird poo? Did a birdie poo on you, Clover?" Skelling tosses her fair curls. "Or is it nits?" she goes on. "Saw your mum checking your hair on your doorstep this morning. You can't wash them out, you know. You have to use special liquid from the chemist that really stinks. Or shave your head." She cackles loudly.

Water dribbles down my back, and the school soap is making my scalp itch. "I don't have nits," I snap.

"Ever seen one under a microscope?" she asks. "They've got massive scratchy claws and pointy mouths to suck your blood."

The bell rings shrilly. "C'mon, Jess, we'd better go," I announce, flinging Skelling a withering look.

"But you're soaking wet," Jess hisses. "You can't go to class like that."

Skelling snorts into her hand. "Better use the hand drier, hadn't you?"

Although I hate to admit it, her suggestion makes more sense than dripping all over the floor in history. I duck under its hot blast with Jess hovering protectively at my side.

"Hurry up," she mutters. "We're going to be late. . ."

"So," Skelling yells over the roar of the dryer, "what kind of *hilarious* costume are you wearing for the carnival this year, Clover?"

"I'm not in it," I yell back.

As far as the carnival's concerned, people either regard it as a huge embarrassment and run riot with water guns, squirting anyone who's dumb enough to have dressed up for the parade. Or they're the idiots *in* the parade. My family belongs to the latter camp. In about six years' time I'll be sitting with a therapist lady who'll say, "Tell me about your childhood, Clover."

And I'll say in a teeny voice: "My mum made me dress up as a burger."

My neck's cricking under the dryer and my head's scorching hot. I'm scared about what'll happen as the oil heats up to an almost unbearable degree. Will I start frying, like a chip? Will I walk into Mr Savage's class with a sizzling head and have to be put out with a fire extinguisher? Hey, that's OK, because olive oil's a *brilliant conditioner.*

Grabbing a fistful of paper towels, I try to blot any remaining damp bits, aware of Skelling's gaze spearing my cheek. "But your family's *always* in it," she insists. "It's one of the highlights of the year. . ."

"Well, we're not doing it any more," I say firmly.

She frowns, seeming in no hurry to go anywhere. "What were you last year?"

"Um, can't remember. . ."

"I do!" she announces. "You were a burger, weren't you? A big brown flat thing between your mum and your sister. Weren't they dressed as . . . buns? Like, half a bun each? And wasn't your dad a bag of *chips*?" She laughs raucously just as Mrs Bryant, the oldest teacher in the known universe, marches in. Her silvery hair is bunned up on her head like a loaf.

"No classes to go to, girls?" she rasps.

"Yes," we all chime, hurrying for the door. Jess and I speed off to history, with me trying to flatten my fluffed-up hair, and Skelling clip-clopping idly behind us.

I'm furious as we march down the corridor. Furious that I never have the guts to stand up to her. "Never let anyone mess you around, Clover," Jupe used to say when we visited. "You've got spirit and heart. Wait until you're let loose on the world. . ." So what happened? No one will notice when I'm "let loose". Or, if they do, they'll laugh their knickers off. Thirteen years old, and Mum rakes through my hair in full view of the street, then sends me to school dripping with oil. And Skelling was right about our carnival costumes – we really did dress up as a burger and buns. The costumes weren't even new or specially made for us. They were part of some publicity stunt that Tony, the chippie owner, dreamed up to attract more customers. I assume he wanted the staff to wear them, but I don't think anyone ever did. Mum found them stuffed in a cupboard in the café kitchen, stinking of grease. She had to wash them before we'd agree to wear them, and even then they *still* reeked.

No wonder Dad's gone. It's obvious now. We're all mad and he couldn't cope with us any longer.

Behind us, Skelling makes a gurgling noise with her throat. You'd never guess one little sound could say so much, but it does.

It says:

Look at the state of you, Clover Jones.

Ever heard of shampoo?

My mum's a fashion designer. She makes underwear for the royal family. That's right – silken knickers for royal derrieres. What does yours do? Oh yeah – she works in a chip shop.

With creepy, greasy Tony.

Maybe she can't afford shampoo.

No wonder your dad ran off.

Did you really think Riley was smiling at you as you were leaving your house this morning?

He was laughing at you, loser, like everyone else in this school.

A lump rises in my throat. Jess catches my eye and smiles encouragingly as we creep into Mr Savage's class. He frowns at us, but thankfully turns back to write on the whiteboard. We're doing the suffragettes. Women who were so desperate to vote and be equal to men that they chained themselves to the railings at 10 Downing Street.

I perch on my chair and pull out my jotters and pencil case. Mr Savage drones on. Outside, pale clouds shift lazily against a turquoise sky. I start imagining Jupe, watching me from somewhere up there, asking why a smart girl like me is so upset by an idiot like Skelling. Did he care if people didn't like his music or wrote bad reviews about his band? Of course he didn't. He didn't care what *anyone* thought, and remembering that makes me feel a whole lot better. "Clover?" Mr Savage's voice snaps me back to reality.

"Yes?" I say quickly.

"Are you with us today? You looked as if you were miles away there."

"Um, sorry," I say. Although my cheeks are burning, I'm actually smiling as Mr Savage turns his attentions back to the suffragettes. It really feels as if my uncle's here, helping me to be strong. *Thanks, Jupe*, I write in the tiniest script on the inside corner of my jotter.

6

Riley Sighting

I manage to avoid any public discussions about Dad by keeping a low profile all morning. By lunchtime, though, there's no chance. Mum spent most of the weekend with the phone jammed at her ear, and gossip spreads like wildfire around Copper Beach. "So, will you have to choose who to live with, Clover?" Amy Sheen bellows in the lunch queue. "Like, go to court and stuff?"

"Of course not," I retort, although I dreamt about that very scenario last night. Only I wasn't me. I was a dog that two people were fighting over, trying to tempt with juicy bones:

Here, Scamp, don't you want to live with me? Look at this bone, yum yum, come and get it. . .

No, you're staying with me, aren't you, Scamp? You don't want bones. We'll build you a lovely new kennel!

"When a couple splits up," Amy jabbers on, "they usually have a custody battle over the kids."

"I . . . er, yeah, I know that." I grip my tray with a plate of dried-up shepherd's pie on it. It's only just happened and I'm already being confronted by custody and courtrooms and old men in curly wigs. Will I have to take an oath and swear on the Bible? I don't even *know* any bits from the Bible.

"Hasn't he gone off with some naked model woman?" she asks eagerly, as if my life were a soap and not horrible, sleazy reality.

"It's kind of private," I snap, grabbing a carton of orange juice.

"What's your mum been like since it happened?"

"Fine, OK?" I say a bit too loudly. It's also a complete lie. Mum might be putting on a brave face, but last night Lily and I peeped out into the back garden and saw her smashing up Dad's tomato plants in the greenhouse.

"Oh well." Amy shrugs and turns away. "I'm sure it'll all work out."

I'm just recovering from this when a tall, gangly figure marches into the canteen. Riley grins when he spots me. "Hey, Clover," he calls out. "Your hair looks nice. Kinda . . . freshly washed."

Brilliant. So Skelling's spread the word about my oil-slick head. "Thanks," I shoot back. "I like to make an effort."

"No, I mean, really." He's closer now, his eyes glinting mischievously. They're a kind of hazelly brown with flecks of amber. There isn't a name for those sort of eyes.

I scrabble for something smart to say. But my mouth won't work, and I'm conscious of a whooshing hotness surging up my neck, as if I'm still trapped underneath the hand dryer.

"Hey, Riley!" Skelling marches in through the door.

He looks round at the sound of her voice. "Got the bird poo out of your hair yet, Clover?" she crows, drawing giggles from around the canteen. I wish Jess were here, but she's gone home for lunch. And I hate myself for needing her.

Riley rolls his eyes at Skelling as he loads up his tray. I don't know why he has this effect on me. He usually has Skelling superglued to his side, which is one major reason to avoid him. Yet he only has to shoot me one of his cheeky looks, and it's like those neon fish from the pet shop are fluttering madly around my insides. Anyway, I *can't* avoid him, as he comes to group guitar lessons every Monday after school. And I'm not giving up those for anyone.

"Hey, Clover," Skelling sneers, following me to an empty table. "There must've been some kind of oil leakage out at sea."

"Give her a break, would you?" Riley says curtly.

"Oh, so you fancy her, do you?" Her eyebrows shoot

upwards, and there's a chorus of laughter from a nearby table.

I sit down and glare at my lunch, realizing, too late, that the pie has something called a "cheese soufflé topping". It looks like hair mousse squirted out of a can.

"OK if I sit here?" Riley asks.

"If you like," I mumble. Riley parks himself beside me, and Skelling nearly sends a gaunt boy in glasses flying as she grabs the seat opposite him. I try a forkful of pie. It slithers, gloop-like, down my throat. There's an awkward silence as Skelling picks at her tuna salad. "You OK, Clover?" Riley asks.

I nod, my stomach swirling uneasily. "Yeah, I'm fine."

"It's just. . ." He pauses, and I can sense him looking at me. I keep my gaze fixed on my hair mousse pie. "I, um, heard about your dad," he adds gently.

Skelling's eyes flick up from her plate. I swivel round to look at him, amazed that he thinks it's OK to bring up such personal stuff in a packed canteen. "Huh?" I say. "What about him?"

"Your dad, I just, um, heard he. . ." Riley tails off and blushes. "Uh, I'm sorry. . ."

"It's got nothing to do with my dad," I snap, taken aback by a surge of anger. "It's just been one of those days, OK? But if you want to gossip about my family, go ahead. I mean, everyone else is. . ." To my horror, my eyes start to flood with tears. Banging down my fork, I stagger up from my seat and blunder towards the canteen door.

"Clover, I didn't mean. . ." Riley protests.

"Whoo, *touchy*!" Skelling yells after me.

7

Malfunctioning Fingers

Having barely recovered from the hair oil and lunch fiasco, I don't feel like going to my guitar lesson at Niall's after school. This is a first. What would Jupe say about that? He'd laugh and puff hard on his roll-up and say, "Jeez, Clover, I can't believe you're giving up because of a *boy*. I thought you were serious about music?" So I *have* to go, obviously.

As we head out of school I say bye to Jess. Then I loiter at the bus stop so Riley's ahead of me and we won't walk down to Niall's together. By the time I get to his house down by the docks, I've managed to convince myself that maybe Riley won't be here this week. "Hi, Clover," Niall says, beckoning me into his tiny fisherman's cottage. "Get yourself sorted; I'll just grab some tea."

"OK." I step meekly into his living room. Damn, Riley's here already.

"Hi," he says awkwardly, glancing up.

"Hi," I say, pulling my guitar out of its case and focusing on tuning it. Normally I can do it without thinking. Niall says I have a brilliant ear. Not today, I don't. Not one string's in tune, no matter how hard I try to concentrate.

"I think your top E's flat," Riley offers helpfully.

"I *know*," I hiss at him. I wish Ben and Kate would turn up so Niall could start our group lesson.

Niall emerges from his kitchen with his customary mug of herbal tea. "Your top E's a bit flat, Clover," he says with a smile, plonking himself on a chair.

I have to hand him my guitar to tune up properly. I can't remember the last time I've had to do that. As Riley flicks through a wad of music, I glance around Niall's living room with a stab of envy. It's so welcoming with its squishy velvet sofa and jewel-coloured wall hangings. The doorbell rings and Kate and Ben tumble in, flushed from the early summer sunshine.

"Sorry we're late," Kate offers.

"Not a problem," Niall says, handing me back my guitar. "Right, everyone, I hope you've practised those bar chords we learnt last week. Want to start, Clover?"

"Um, OK." I try to form the right shapes with the fingers of my left hand. *Think. Think.* Nothing comes. My fingers feel like limp sausages. Riley's lunchtime comment rings in my head: *I heard about your dad. . .* And Amy's: *Will you have to go to court?* Should I just put a full-page announcement in the *Copper Beach Gazette*?

NEWSFLASH! Clover Jones's dad now lives with a nudie model. Buy your copy tomorrow for the next thrilling instalment!

Tears prickle my eyes and I blink them away. Riley shuffles in his seat.

"Clover?" Niall says gently. "Everything OK?"

"I, um, I can't remember the chords," I mutter.

"Well, never mind," he says quickly. "Bar chords are pretty tricky at first, but you'll soon pick them up. I'll run through them with you again, all right?"

"Thanks," I say, furious with myself for being so useless. Jupe taught me so much that Niall often asks me to show Riley, Kate and Ben how it's done. And I usually love these lessons. It feels so good, being able to do something easily. Now the others are waiting patiently as Niall gently manoeuvres my fingers into position. But they *still* won't work. First my ears, now my fingers. It's as if my body's falling to pieces, bit by bit.

Twaaaang! My strings ring out, discordant and ugly. Riley shoots me a concerned frown. Niall tries again and again until there's no option but to give up and carry on with the lesson.

I can't even play the songs we learnt weeks ago. You'd never believe Jupe taught me to play when I was seven years old.

Then my D string breaks and there's no time to put on another one before the end of the lesson. I zip my guitar into its case, keeping my eyes lowered. "See you all next week," Niall says brightly as his wife pads downstairs with Miles, their snoozing baby son. How has he managed to nap with the awful racket I've been making? Maybe he willed himself to sleep to escape from the horror of it all.

We all step out into the cobbled courtyard. It's drizzling now, and the sky's turned moody grey. "Hey Clover," Niall calls from the doorway. "Everyone has their off days, you know? Don't stress about it."

I nod glumly.

"Maybe you've got other stuff on your mind, huh?"

"Kind of."

"Chin up," he says kindly. "See you next week."

By the time I head for the high street, the others have disappeared. Then I spot Riley, waiting for me. "Hey," he says, smiling.

I nod curtly. Gripping my guitar case tightly and trying my best to ignore the dancing fish in my belly, I walk on by.

"Hey, Clover! What's the hurry?" Riley calls out, scuttling after me into the busy street.

"I need to get home," I snap. I don't really, not today. Usually, I have to pick up Lily from her gym class after guitar, but today she's going to her friend Hannah's. Mum will be working till six, so there's nothing to rush home for.

Riley falls into step with me but keeps pinging me quizzical looks. His school sweatshirt's knotted around his waist, and he's wearing a creamy-coloured T-shirt that's close enough to our regulation polo shirts for him to get away with it.

I walk faster, keeping my expression as frosty as possible.

"Look," he says, a little out of breath, "I'm really sorry about what I said at lunchtime. Mentioning your parents, I mean. It was really stupid. . ."

"S'OK," I growl.

"I . . . I should know better," he adds, " 'cause I've been through it too."

I flick a look at him. For one dumb moment I assume he means his dad ran off with a nudie model too. "I mean my parents broke up," Riley adds.

I stop and look at him. "Did they? I never knew that." I assumed I knew everything about Riley Hart, or at least the important stuff: the way he tosses his fair fringe from his eyes and how it flips straight back again. How his cheeks dimple when he laughs, and the back of his neck turns gingerbread-brown in the sun. How he tries and tries in Niall's lessons, but messes up every time.

And how he makes me go fizzy inside.

"About a year and a half ago," he continues, "just before Christmas. Great timing, huh? All my aunties and uncles had come to stay. . ." He shrugs, meeting my gaze, starting the fish going crazy in my stomach.

"That must've been awful," I say.

"Well, I guess it's never the right time, is it? But you do get used to things being different."

I turn this over in my mind. Not worse – just different. Will I ever be able to think of it like that? "D'you live with your mum?" I ask.

He shakes his head. "No, with my dad. Mum went away for a week to London. Well, it was meant to be a week – she told Dad she needed to 'find herself'." He smirks. "A week, can you believe that? It used to take her three days to find her car keys."

I smile, despite the awfulness of my day. "*Did* she find herself?"

"No, but she found a new boyfriend. Some guy called Mike who seemed to sort out her chakras or whatever they're called."

"God," I murmur. He's sharing all this as we cross the high street, and I marvel at how he can turn sad stuff on its head and squeeze the funniness out of it. We fall silent for a few moments; then I sense him looking at me. "You'll be all right next week," he adds.

"Will I?" I exclaim.

"I didn't mean about your dad," he adds quickly. "I mean at Niall's, with those bar chords and everything. . ."

"Oh. Yeah, probably."

"You're heaps better than the rest of us," he continues. "You make it look so easy, as if your fingers do what you want without you having to even think . . . it's just so natural with you."

I splutter with laughter. "Not today, it wasn't."

He tilts his head and smiles. It's the kind of smile that

makes me forget everything for a moment: Mum, Dad, even the olive oil fiasco this morning. "We all have our off days," he adds.

We've wound up outside Tony's chippie. Through the steamed-up window I can make out Mum, chatting across the counter to a customer. I can see why Tony rates her. She makes people feel welcome, with all her smiles and chat, whereas Tony acts like he'd rather work in a mortuary than his own restaurant.

"Doesn't your mum work in here?" Riley asks. So he knows *details* about me. This makes me feel very weird.

"Uh-huh," I say.

"C'mon, I'm starving. Would she give us some chips, d'you think?"

"No, Tony would go mad!" That's not true. Tony's usually so busy snarling over the fryer, he doesn't notice if Mum dishes out a few freebies. It's the thought of her smirking at us, then firing questions and teasing me when she gets home.

Riley frowns. "You don't want your mum to see you with me? Is that it?"

"Of course not," I protest.

"Great. In fact, I've probably got enough money for two portions anyway. C'mon, let's get out of this rain."

I'm about to say it's only drizzle, and wouldn't we be better getting bags of chips to eat outside? But Riley's already marched in, swinging his guitar, and is ordering two platefuls at the counter.

Mum's all sparkly as she serves us. "Aren't you going to introduce me to your friend, Clover?" she prompts me, beaming at Riley.

"Um, this is Riley, he goes to guitar lessons. . ." I mumble.

"Hi, Riley," she says, smiling. She's looking better already, and is even wearing mascara, which is starting to smudge in the heat.

Riley and I grab the only free table, which happens to be at the window. I'd rather have hidden away at the back. What if Skelling or one of her buddies walks by and spots us? I know if she sees us, she'll come stomping right in and bring up my hair oil incident or start making sneery remarks about my weird family. And I just want a few minutes with Riley all to myself.

He chuckles.

"What's funny?" I ask.

"That sign," he says, pointing. It's pinned up wonkily behind the counter and says: *Smiles cost nothing so we give them for free.*

"You know what?" I say. "I've never actually seen Tony smile. I don't know how Mum stands it in here."

"Well, *I* like it," Riley says firmly. "Maybe we could do this again after next week's lesson. Or sooner, if you're not doing anything. . ." His words come out all bunched up together.

"I usually have to look after Lily after school," I say

quickly. "The only reason I can come to guitar lessons is because she's at gym."

Riley nibbles a chip. "Well, maybe I could come round to yours sometime to practise guitar? Would that be OK?"

I hesitate. There are so many reasons why he can't come – like the fact that Skelling would probably prise out my eyeballs and stamp on them. "What about Sophie?"

There. I've said it.

Riley shrugs. "What about her?"

"Well, she's always with you, isn't she? And I wondered. . ."

"I can do what I like," he says with a shrug. "Sophie doesn't own me."

"I know, but. . ."

"Anyway," he cuts in, "all these lessons I'm having with Niall. . . I'm just not getting any better, you know? It's like some kind of mental block. Maybe you could help me before my dad decides it's a waste of money and stops me going? Would you do that?"

His eyes hold mine for a moment. I know he's not asking me out or anything, and it really *is* just a guitar thing between us. But still, I feel the grin spreading like honey across my face. "Sure," I say. "That'd be good."

"Shall we swap numbers then?"

I nod, glancing up at Tony's sign, while trying to blot

out Mum, who's winking at me. Smiles *are* free, I think crazily. I'm bursting with them.

My ears and fingers might have malfunctioned today. But my heart, which is flipping delightedly as I pull out my phone, seems to be working just fine.

Jurassic Burgers

"Clover! *Clover!*" comes the voice next lunchtime as Jess and I head towards the canteen. "Clover, over here!"

I peer across the yard towards the railings, aware of the blood draining from my face. It's Dad, standing and waving in full view of everyone. "What's he doing here?" Jess gasps.

"No idea," I hiss as Skelling and her fans skitter past us, giggling away.

With a deep breath and my chin held high, I march towards him. Whatever it is, I hope it's going to be quick. I feel more than a little weird about Dad right now. Now I realize that Lily's jammed next to him, with a grin plastered all over her face too. Despite the fact that he's abandoned us, she's obviously delighted to see him. Right now, I don't know *what* I am.

"Hi, Clover," Dad says, reaching out for a hug.

"Hullo, Dad." I stand, rigid as a drainpipe, waiting

for the hug to finish. It feels like billions of eyes are stabbing the back of my head.

"Thought I'd treat my girls to a special lunch," he announces, releasing me from his grasp.

"Why?" I ask. Dad has never treated us to a "special lunch".

He shuffles awkwardly and takes Lily's hand. "I just think we need to have a talk."

"But you can't just take Lily out like this!" I protest. "She has school lunches, remember? The teachers'll be wondering where she's gone. . ."

"I sorted all that," he says calmly. "Called the school office, said I was coming to collect her for lunch."

"Oh," I mutter.

"Haven't got much time, though, have we? God, they work you kids hard." His face cracks into another smile. "Come on, love, let's go."

"But, Dad, I was going to have lunch with Jess and I don't really want. . ." I glance back at her and she shrugs. It's no good. Obviously, whatever Dad has in mind is more important than my lunchtime arrangements.

It turns out that our "special lunch" is at Dinosaur Diner down at the seafront.

There are colour-in place mats depicting prehistoric scenes, and packets of fat wax crayons laid out on the tables. Even Lily's outgrown colour-in place mats, but is dutifully shading in the spikes on a stegosaurus's back.

I reckon she has an invisible shell to protect herself,

a bit like those dinosaurs had. Since Dad walked out on Saturday she's tried to act as if nothing's changed – babbling on about chocolate fountains and chatting on the phone to her friends. I know, though, that it does bother her really. She's meant to be making a collage for her Brownie artist badge on the theme of "my family". Ages ago, she cut out little paper drawings of us. Now, whenever she tries to make us into a collage, she sits surrounded by all these paper figures, as if she can no longer work out where to put anyone.

"So!" Dad says overeagerly. "What d'you fancy, girls?" He grips an enormous laminated menu with cartoon dinosaurs dancing all over it.

I skim the options. Nothing has an ordinary name. You don't get a burger and fries, you get a *Tyrannosaurus Burger and Jurassic Sizzlers.* It's not a side order of coleslaw, but *Munchy-Crunchy Herbivore Slaw Bursting With Essential Vits.* I'll tell you what's bursting. My brain, from answering Dad's lame questions about homework and guitar lessons and has Betty next door got a new cat to replace Midnight yet? As if he's been gone for months, not three days. What I'd really love is to be in Horsedung's canteen right now, and I *never* thought I'd say that.

"Um, everything OK at school, Clover?" Dad asks.

"Yeah," I say firmly. I don't mention my oil-slick disaster yesterday, or Amy going on about courts and judges and all that stuff. I don't bring up any of that because what could Dad do about it anyway? So there's no point.

Anyway, what's happened to our big talk that Dad seemed so keen to have? Maybe he's forgotten, or is trying to communicate telepathically. I try to tune into his thought-waves, but can only pick up someone yelling in the kitchen.

We order our food, which arrives almost instantly. My burger tastes of shoe. Maybe it really is Jurassic. "Isn't this great?" Dad says, looking desperate.

I scowl at him. My fingers seized up at my guitar lesson and now my throat's gone weird as well. "Will I have to go to court, Dad?" I blurt out suddenly.

"*What?*" He blinks at me, horrified. Lily gawps at Dad, clutching a limp chip.

"Go to court," I repeat, steadying my voice. "Isn't that what happens when people get divorced?"

Dad reaches for my hand across the sticky table. I shouldn't want him to hold it, but I do. "What's put that into your head, sweetheart?" he asks softly.

"Who's going to court?" Lily demands.

"Er, someone at school mentioned it," I babble, "and I just thought. . ."

"Listen," Dad insists. "Nothing like that's going to happen, OK? No one's going to court. You'll both stay with Mum, and we'll make arrangements so we can get together every weekend and do nice things like come here for lunch. . ."

A fossilized lump has jammed in my throat.

"...And maybe I'll bring Bernice so you can see how nice she is. That's why I wanted to see you. To explain everything to my favourite girls."

Bernice. The word hovers awkwardly between us. I take a gulp of Coke to try and dislodge the lump.

"Would you like that?" Dad asks.

"Yes, Dad," Lily says quietly, looking down at her place mat. She knows who Bernice is. Mum has spat out the word enough times on the phone.

"Clover?" Dad prompts me.

"Uh-huh."

"You'd be OK with that?"

"I suppose so." What else can I say?

He frowns, trying to make eye contact. I stare down at the cartoon pterodactyls on the menu. "Like some pudding?" he asks when we've all made half-hearted attempts at our main courses.

"Sorry," I say quickly, "but we need to get back."

"Oh, of course." Had he forgotten about school, or what? Doesn't he care about our *education*?

We drop off Lily and I say a speedy goodbye to Dad. "I'll have to run to make it back for the bell," I say, dodging his kiss.

I pelt along, my hair flying. Since Dad left, I've spent every spare moment playing guitar to try and take my mind off what's happened. Sometimes it's worked. I've lost myself in the songs, just like when it was Jupe and me. Now, though, Dad's stormed back into my head. And he lied, I figure as Horsedung looms into view, about me and Lily being his favourite girls. That woman is now.

Nudie Bernice.

She's his number one.

"Hey, where were you at lunchtime?" comes the voice behind me. I swing round, steadying my breath from my run. Riley looks like he's been running too. "I, er, had to . . . meet someone," I say.

"Oh." He looks lost for a moment, then adds, "You know you said you'd help me with guitar?"

"Uh-huh. . ." My Dad-induced mood lifts a little, although the burger taste still lurks in my throat.

"All right if I come over later today?" Riley asks.

I pause for a moment, wondering if I should pretend to be busy, just so I don't seem too keen. But after that dismal lunch with Dad, what would be nicer than hanging out with Riley for a couple of hours? "Sure," I say lightly as we step into school together. "That'd be cool."

9

Shaky Wet Dog Music

"I'd really appreciate it," I tell Lily as we walk home, "if you'd give me and Riley some privacy and not hang about, sticking your nose in."

"Why?" she asks, frowning.

"Because . . . there's stuff he wants me to show him on guitar and he'll be embarrassed if you're there."

"Why? D'you fancy him?"

"Course not! He's just a boy from school, all right?"

She shoots me a sly look. "Have you kissed him?"

"Oh, for God's sake." I start to walk faster so she has to scurry along to keep up. It's not normal to have to spend as much time with your little sister as I do. Unless I'm at school, she's there, pinging questions at me. I officially have *no* life.

"So what am I meant to do," she asks, "while you're. . . *showing him stuff*?"

"Stay out of the bedroom," I say firmly.

"That's not fair! It's my room too. I'll just sit and draw in the corner and be quiet."

"But you'd still be there," I point out. "You'd still be *breathing*. Can't you watch telly or something?"

She blasts out a huge groan and lets her camouflage school bag slip from her shoulder and drag along the ground, narrowly missing a spillage of curry. "Sorr*eee*!" she sing-songs. "I won't breathe, then. I'll stop breathing and die and *then* you'll be sorry."

Sometimes I think my heart's like a guitar string, because it twangs with guilt when she says stuff like that. I glare at Lily. We've shared a room since she was born. When she was old enough she'd climb out of her cot while I was asleep, and I'd wake up with her snuggled up next to me in bed, gusting milk breath in my face.

That was OK. Now I'm not so keen on sharing. The only place I get any privacy to read the magazines Jess gives me is on the loo with the door locked. We must be the only family in the developed world without a computer, so I can't read stuff online. I'm not even safe in the bathroom. If I'm more than three minutes, Mum starts hammering on the door, shouting, "What are you *doing* in there?" as if I might be slathering myself with her precious wrinkle creams.

I glower at Lily. "I'll pay you," I mutter.

"How much?" Her eyes gleam like wet pebbles.

"Fifty pence."

"That's not enough! I want at least a pound. *Two* pounds."

I snort in acknowledgement of being ripped off, but agree because I feel light and excited about Riley coming over. My head whirls with things to show him, like how to strum like you mean it and not sound afraid. Focusing on guitar-things is dampening my nervousness.

But as we turn into our road, my stomach tightens again. Our house is practically quaking with deafening rock music. We can hear it from the far end of the street. Mum plays this stuff when she's worked up about something, so I know things are bad.

She likes terrible bands from when she was young. Bands who wear tight, shiny trousers and have masses of hair which they shake madly like wet dogs. OK, Jupe had a few pairs of scarily tight trousers stashed in his wardrobe. But he wrote *songs*, proper music that meant something to people. These other bands Mum likes just roar and wail as if they're in agony.

I push open our front door and pause. "Why's Mum home?" Lily shouts over the music. "Shouldn't she be at work?"

"Don't know. Maybe she's sick and came home early." But this isn't sick-bed music. Dumping my bag in the hall, I march in.

"Hi girls!" Mum's stirring something tomatoey in a pan on the hob. "Good day at school?"

"Um, yes," I yell back, deciding not to mention our

jolly lunch with Dad. "Why are you home? Haven't you been at work?"

"I quit," she announces.

"Did you get the sack?" Lily asks brightly.

"No, sweetheart. I said *quit*. Big difference. Hang on a minute and I'll turn the music down." She does – a bit – but it's still pretty loud compared to what you'd hear in any normal house.

"But why?" I ask when she comes back into the kitchen.

She sucks in a huge breath, as if the extra oxygen might help her explain. Her lipstick and eyeshadow look creased and end-of-day-ish. "You know Tony, my boss?" she says.

I nod.

"Well. . ." She flicks her gaze at Lily. "He, um . . . now I'm single and all on my own without a man or anything . . . he seemed to get. . ." She blushes and laughs awkwardly, showing her small, even teeth. "The wrong idea about me and him," she finishes in a gallop.

"*What* wrong idea?" Lily asks.

Mum turns back to the bubbling pot. "The idea that I might want to, er . . . you know. Be his, um . . . *girlfriend*."

"Ugh," I shudder. Is that what happens when your husband leaves you? You're slobbered over by men with fat, sweaty faces and enormous pink arms? Tony is *gross.*

"Anyway," she goes on, "I was sick of having stinky hair and giving smiles for free. The only trouble is, now we won't be able to borrow those costumes from the chippie for the carnival."

The carnival! The very word pierces my heart. "What about money?" I ask, trailing after Mum as she removes the CD from the player and pops in another.

"We'll manage," she says. I'm about to ask *how will we manage exactly?* when there's a sharp knocking on our front door.

Riley. Oh God. I'd been looking forward to him coming over all afternoon and now I can't imagine anything worse. He *can't* come in. Not with Mum's music on, which I'm sure she'll turn up to top volume again at any moment. We won't be able to hear ourselves play, for a start. And he'll decide Mum's mad and tell everyone and never speak to me ever again. "Answer the door!" I hiss at Lily. "If it's Riley, tell him I'm not in."

She blinks at me. "What should I say?"

"Just tell him I've had to go out!"

"But why?" Lily's forehead wrinkles in confusion.

"Tell who?" Mum asks.

"Just . . . a boy." My heart's banging so fiercely, I'm surprised she can't hear it.

"That nice boy you had chips with?" Mum says with a smirk.

I nod. There's another loud knock.

"Let him in!" Lily demands, no doubt thinking about her two quid.

I glare at her. "No. I don't want to see him, OK?

Please, Lily. Go tell him . . . our dog's escaped and I've gone out looking for him."

"For goodness' sake, Clover," Mum guffaws.

"But we don't *have* a dog," Lily yells after me as I hurtle up to our bedroom.

I perch on the edge of my bed, feeling faintly sick with Jurassic whiffs still burping up from my stomach. There's more knocking, then another song starts up – louder this time – and I can just make out the front door being opened and Lily roaring something over the racket. I wonder what Riley will make of it. He'll probably think it's a family passion, and that I secretly love this kind of music too.

And he'll think, God, and I actually *liked* Clover Jones, for about four minutes. Close call.

After a few moments, I creep to the window. A long-legged figure is crossing the road. He stops to glance back at our house, and I lurch away. What I really want to do is throw the window open and yell, "Riley! I'm sorry, OK? I'll explain everything tomorrow. And please believe me that I *don't like this music*. . ." But I can't because Dad painted the window frame shut and even if he hadn't, I'd never dare.

Riley's walking faster now, swinging his guitar, and then he turns the corner out of sight.

Lily's face pops round our bedroom door. She pads over to my bed and perches on its edge beside me. "Why didn't you let Riley come in?" she asks. "Don't you like him any more?"

"Leave me alone," I growl.

Her face clouds, and she stomps over to our wardrobe and performs a handstand against it. I can sense her scrutinizing me from her upside-down position. Trying to blot her out, I curl up on my bed and delve around my brain for some comforting thoughts. Like that guitar lesson with Niall when I picked up new chords first time and he asked me to help everyone else. Or eating chips with Riley, and steamy vinegar smells drifting around us.

Why did he want to come over, anyway? He probably does just want help with his guitar, which is fine, I guess. Maybe his dad's been threatening to stop his lessons unless he improves. Or perhaps he's trying to make Skelling jealous. They walk to school together, after all, and she's always hanging around him like a bad smell. There's no way he doesn't fancy her. *All* the boys do.

"Clover," Lily pipes up, flipping back on to her feet, "will I still get my two pounds?"

"What for?" I retort.

"You said you'd pay me if I left you alone with Riley."

"But he didn't come in! You didn't have to do anything!"

"Yes I did. I answered the door and I lied. I said you were out walking Bambi."

"Bambi?" I splutter. "Who's Bambi?"

"Our dog." She grins.

"We don't have a dog," I protest, "and if we did, we wouldn't call it Bambi. . ."

"But you told me to say we had one! If we did, what would we call it?"

"I don't know! Um. . ." I try to think of acceptable pets' names but all I can dredge up is Cedric, our hamster, and Jupe's mean old cat, Fuzz.

"I still want my two pounds," Lily says firmly.

With a cursory snort I reach for my purse, delve through the pathetic remains of my birthday money after buying Ced's tunnel, and fish out a two-pound coin.

Lily studies it as if it were a jewel. "Thanks. Can we draw now? Please, Clover?"

Mum's put on another CD, so there isn't much else I can do while my brain's being destroyed by wailing guitars and cringey lyrics. "OK," I say reluctantly.

Lily rummages for paper and pens in our cupboard. "Will you show me how to draw a giraffe?" she demands.

"I'll try." We sprawl on the carpet to draw pictures, although I'm finding it hard to be artistic after what's just happened.

"That's not a giraffe," Lily scoffs. "It looks like a table with a neck."

I try not to laugh but it bursts out of me anyway, and

soon we're both sniggering, drawing dumb pictures of furniture made into animals. Lily's taking my mind off Riley Hart, at least. I suppose I should be grateful for that. Although it's hardly worth two blinking quid.

10

Teary Girlie Outburst

Skelling swished into school with a dramatic new hairstyle this morning. The yellowy curls had gone, and it sprung around her cheeks in honeyish layers. Although it kills me to admit it, the transformation was magical. "Mum let me go to the Cutting Room," I heard her bragging at break. "I know it's heaps of money, but if you pay peanuts you get monkeys cutting your hair, know what I mean?"

And it set an idea smouldering in my head. If I'm going to keep my promise to Jupe and form a band, I can't have a sad, straggly haircut, can I? I'm a teenager now, and should look like one. So I decide to broach the subject with Mum.

I wait until after dinner. Mum and I are washing up while Lily de-festers Cedric's cage in the back garden.

"That Riley boy seemed nice," Mum muses. "Are you going to ask him over again?"

"Maybe," I say with a shrug.

"And maybe you'll actually invite him in next time," she teases. "What happened – did you have a shyness attack or something?"

"Something like that," I say quickly, drying a pasta bowl vigorously.

"Well," Mum says, tossing back her hair, "he must like you. You were a bit rude, Clover."

How can I tell her that it would have been pointless anyway, with her blasting that music of hers? It would have been awful. Mum gets all excited when people come over and would probably have started *dancing*. I can feel her scrutinizing me, as if she wants to say something else, and is mulling over the best way to put it. It hovers between us like an invisible cloud.

I pray that she's not about to divulge further details about Tony – that he's come round to see her and tried to plant a fishy-lipped kiss on her face. I'm still having a hard time coping with the idea of Dad and Nudie Bernice. Mum smiles and pushes my fringe out of my eyes. "You need a trim, love," she says.

"Yeah, I know." I hesitate, wondering how to bring this up. My thinking goes this way: if I ask for a trim at the Cutting Room, and not a hugely expensive cut-and-colour job like Skelling's, I'll actually be *saving* us money.

"I don't know how you can see where you're going," Mum jokes.

Do it. Ask. She's practically fed you the line. "Um, could I have my hair done at the Cutting Room?" I blurt out.

Mum blinks at me. "What, that new place by the Odeon?"

"Yeah."

"Are you out of your mind, Clover Jones? I've just walked out on my job, if you hadn't noticed. D'you know what I've had to put up with, with Tony's wandering hands?"

"Mum, I—" I start.

"Have you any idea how much they charge in there? I bet it's three quid for a cup of tea before they've even picked up a pair of scissors!"

"I-I don't want tea," I stammer. "I wouldn't have anything to drink. . ."

"I'll get Babs to come over," she says firmly. "I'm sure she'll manage to squeeze you in before the carnival."

My heart dive-bombs. For years, Lily and I have had our hair cut and "styled" – I use the term loosely – by Mum's friend Babs. She makes random stabbing motions while swigging red wine and chatting the whole time to Mum. I could lose an ear, an eye, anything. I'm sure there's a law against being drunk and in charge of sharp scissors.

"I was thinking, though," I stumble on, "that just for a change, could I go to a proper hairdresser?"

"Babs is a proper hairdresser," Mum says with a frown. "She trained at a top London salon, remember?"

"Yeah, about thirty years ago," I snap.

Mum peers at me. "So what? She's experienced.

What's got into you, Clover? D'you think I'm made of money? Don't you know the stress I've been through lately?"

I stare at her, watching her mouth moving, no longer listening to what she's saying. Then, with my eyes brimming with tears, I hurtle into the living room, let out a demented wail and belly-flop on to the sofa.

I'm crying and snivelling on to our velvety cushions. Who cares if I make them wet and snotty and am being horribly immature? I'm sick of this. Sick of being Clover Jones with mad parents and flumpy hair and having to draw giraffes. I'm thirteen! Isn't that meant to be some kind of milestone? Isn't your mum meant to take you out to buy pretty lacy bras instead of horrible cropped vesty things, and let you have a proper haircut that's not done by a drunk maniac with grey teeth? (Fact: red wine turns your teeth grey. Weird, I know. You'd expect them to go red. Even weirder, it makes your lips black, which is *such* a great look for a top London salon-trained hairdresser, I always think. Miaow.) Anyway, if Babs is so great, how come last time she coloured Mum's hair she left a beetrooty tidemark on her forehead?

Mum stomps into the living room and glares at me. "All I mean is," she says in a calmer voice, "Lily doesn't ask me for forty-quid haircuts and guitar lessons and God knows what else. . ."

"It doesn't matter," I mutter.

"Anyway," she adds, looking slightly uncomfortable now, "seeing as we're on the subject of guitar lessons, Clover, I'm sorry, but I can't afford them any more."

I spring up from the sofa and blink at her. "What? What d'you mean?"

She sighs and her face softens. "Look, love, I know it doesn't seem like much, but now I'm not working we'll all have to pull together as a family."

"D'you mean . . . I have to stop?" I ask faintly. "Please, Mum, I. . ."

"Not for ever," she interrupts. "I'm not saying that. But you'll have to put them on hold until I have a job sorted out. I know your dad's paying the rent, and he says he won't see us go short, but there's nothing left for extras at the moment. . ."

"My guitar lessons aren't extras!" I shriek. "It's the only thing I do! Some people go to drama workshop and ice skating and I don't do any of that. I've always come home and looked after Lily. . ."

"You don't mind doing that, do you? Looking after your sister, I mean?"

I glance at the door, my heart thudding furiously. Lily has wandered in from the garden and is staring at us. "*Do* you, Clover?" my sister breathes, clasping Cedric's cage to her chest.

"No," I say gruffly. "Of course I don't." I stare down at our worn carpet, conscious of both of them staring at me. Obviously, Mum's gym membership and wrinkle creams don't count as "extras". And we're not talking cheap brands, *oh* no, unless it's hospital shampoo for me and Lily. I bet one pot of Mum's eye cream would convert into at least five lessons with Niall. I've even spotted special moisturizing bubble bath with real gold particles floating in it. How much did *that* cost? Why does anyone need real gold in their bath? Obviously it's more important for Mum to stay skinny and obliterate her non-existent wrinkles than for me to be a brilliant guitarist.

My brain buzzes with possible solutions. I could save up for tutor books and teach myself – but you need to be shown by a real person, or at least I do. Niall shares musicians' secrets, stuff you'd never learn from books. He's so patient, too, and makes me want to get better, just like Jupe did. Can't she understand that I *need* him?

"Couldn't I have a lesson every two weeks?" I ask, desperation creeping into my voice.

"Clover," Mum sounds exasperated now, "I've tried to explain, OK? There must be free music lessons at school."

"Only trumpet and trombone. . ."

"Then why can't you—"

"I don't want to play the stupid trombone!" I yell, grabbing and flinging the first thing within reach, which happens to be a damp tea towel draped over the radiator. See what a pathetic specimen I am? I don't smash glasses or plates. I don't fling TVs through the window like rock stars did back in Jupe's day.

No, I throw a tea towel with little birdies on it. Whoo, *scary.*

Sellotape and Scissors

In the sanctuary of my bedroom, my breathing comes ragged and tight. I *won't* stop going to Niall's. There must be something I can do. I yank my guitar from its case and try to play something soothing, but had forgotten that I still haven't got around to replacing the broken string because I don't have enough money to buy new ones. And I know how Mum'd react if I asked her. How many strings could you buy in exchange for one bottle of gold-particle bubble bath?

I play anyway, wondering if Dad would donate some money to the cause – at least for new strings. He's phoned me a couple of times, just to ask about school and Cedric and nothingy stuff. But I'm scared to call him, even on his mobile, in case Nudie Bernice picks it up. What would I say? What if she tried to make friends with me and invited me over for tea or something? Sometimes, when Dad's name comes up on my mobile and I don't feel like I can pretend I'm OK, I just let it go to voicemail instead.

"What's a trombone?" Lily asks, sauntering into our bedroom.

I carry on strumming, trying to blot out the dangling broken string that I haven't even got around to taking off.

"I said *what's a trombone*?"

"It's like a trumpet with a long slidey thing," I mutter.

"What kind of slidey thing?"

"Like this," I say, performing a half-hearted mime.

"Oh, I know! Like those old-man bands at the seafront. Why don't you want—"

"I don't want to play in an old-man band, OK?"

She frowns. "But I only—"

"Why does everyone want me to play trombone?" I yell. Lily's face droops. "Sorry," I sigh. "Me and Mum, we just had a . . . a *thing*. . ."

"S'all right," she mumbles, chewing a fingernail. Now I feel rotten. None of this is her fault. She's only eight – what does she care about my guitar lessons? Her life revolves around sleepovers and gaining her next Brownie badge. And she's right – why shouldn't I learn the stupid trombone? I can see myself now, marching through town in a brass-buttoned uniform with a drum being whacked in my earhole. That'd give Skelling something to snort about. More, even, than olive oil day, or my appearance as a hamburger in last year's carnival. I can picture her and Riley having a right old laugh over that.

"What was the thing about anyway?" Lily ventures.

"Oh, just me, explaining that I don't want Babs to do my hair any more. . ."

"*I* like Babs cutting my hair," Lily says.

"Yeah, but only because she gives you chocolate."

"Lily!" Mum calls upstairs. "Lily, darling, how d'you fancy making us all some cookies?"

Ha! So Mum's trying to redeem herself by baking doughy lumps that even the birds will reject. "OK, Mum," Lily calls back, giving me a confused look before bounding out of our room. Obviously, Mum's Cookies of Doom are preferable to my brooding presence.

I'm relieved Lily's gone. Now I can examine myself in our dressing table mirror and figure out a plan. Whilst I can't do much about the guitar situation, I *can* try to fix my appearance, which is particularly tragic today. My skin's not bad – creamy pale with a faint scattering of toffee-coloured freckles – and my eyebrows are nicely curved and kind of graceful. But who gets excited over *eyebrows*? Anyway, my hair's so overgrown you can't even see them. I pick up a wodge of fringe and let it drop. "She trained at a top London salon!" I crow into the mirror. "D'you think I'm made of money?"

Mum said herself that I can hardly see where I'm going. Doesn't she care that I could walk smack-bang into a lamp post and get concussion and damage my brain? Something catches my eye on our desk. Scissors. It's easy to cut your own fringe. I read about it in one of

Jess's magazines. They even had step-by-step pictures showing you exactly what to do. OK, they were only drawings, and things never go wrong in drawings (unless you're trying to draw a giraffe, obviously). But it still looked less traumatic than having a drunk maniac blasting her wine breath in your face.

All you do is stick a strip of tape across your forehead and snip along the line. Why can you never find any Sellotape in our house? I rummage through mine and Lily's desk drawers and chaotic cupboard. Out falls a pile of Lily's old drawings. Most are of cats – ginger cats, tabby cats and Midnight, Betty's moggy that got run over by a delivery lorry on Christmas Eve. R.I.P. MIDNIGHT, she's written. Angel wings sprout from his back. Poor, sweet Midnight who loved me and Lil.

There's one drawing that's not of a cat, but a girl (although her green eyes are distinctly feline). She has thick dark hair and a guitar strapped across her body. It's me – at least, a flattering version of me. I look determined, verging on fierce. The kind of girl who might throw a spectacular tantrum, not a damp tea towel with birdie-wirdies on it.

Underneath her drawing, Lily has written: *For my sister Clover.*

I blink at it, and my insides twist with shame. She wouldn't want to draw me now as I unearth the Sellotape from the back of the cupboard and press a strip across my fringe (or at least, where my new-improved fringe will finish). I'm pretty certain that Skelling's never been driven to such desperate measures.

I grab the scissors and take a massive breath for courage. I'm not even sure I've got the Sellotape straight, which doesn't bode well for the cutting part, but I'm too charged up now to stop. Maybe I *can* do this. I could start trimming fringes at school for guitar lesson money, working up to whole haircuts. I picture my own salon, with "Clover's Cuts" painted in elaborate purple swirly writing above the window. I'd treat customers to posh herbal teas instead of the builder's type Mum drinks. *And* all the drinks would be free. Once business was flourishing, I'd start styling models' hair for magazines, which would be ironic, as Mum thinks magazines are a waste of money (like guitar lessons and proper haircuts). And all the time I'd have my band and we'd rehearse and rehearse until we were ready to play live and I'd hand over Clover's Cuts to a trusted friend like Jess.

Mum's voice drifts upstairs: "Thanks, Lily, you're being so *helpful* today! Don't these cookies smell good? Are they ready, d'you think?"

I hear a metal tray being set down on the worktop and the pair of them chatting excitedly. Mum's right, they *do* smell good. Not like the last batch, which she incinerated because she was too busy playing her music at top volume. "Let's try them," Lily says.

There's silence, then Mum says, "What d'you think? Better than the last lot, aren't they?"

My stomach rumbles. Mum and Lily are down there, munching warm cookies, having a lovely time without me. Focusing on the wonky Sellotape, I lunge towards my reflection and start to cut.

12

Beauty Tip 2: *Definitely* Don't Try This at Home

The *scccrrrunch* of the scissors is weirdly satisfying.

Scccrrrunch.

Scccrrrunch.

Scccrrrunch. It's rhythmic and soothing. In fact, I'm so wrapped up in what I'm doing, I'm almost sorry when it's time to stop.

Then I peel off the Sellotape, and . . . *Jesus.*

I don't mean I *look* like Jesus, because in pictures I've seen he's had long, wavy hair – pretty cool hair, actually, for a guy who was kicking around about two thousand years ago. I mean, half the boys who hang out at the North Cove have Jesus-y hair. But no one has hair like *this.*

It's all up-and-down wonky, as if I've hacked at it blindfolded with plastic round-ended scissors. Even Drunk Babs wouldn't inflict this on a person. Sweat springs from my brow as I shut my eyes tight. When I open them again, my fringe hasn't miraculously straightened itself. How has this happened? Stupid magazine! My eyes look dark and scared. I know the tape was a bit skewed to start with, but it wasn't *this* bad. Do we have mutant Sellotape? I pull another strip off the roll and hold it taut. Nope, it's straight all right. That means it's *me* that's wobbly.

"Clover!" Mum calls from the kitchen. "Come down, would you, love?"

Love. I'm back in favour, obviously – at least until she sees this. My whole body tenses with fear. "OK, just a minute," I call back in a strained voice.

Abandoning the tape method, I cut another line into my fringe. Now it looks as if it's been attacked by rusty garden shears.

"Clover!" Mum shouts. "Hurry up. We've got something to show you."

My heart thuds. Do I have something to show *her.*

OK, keep calm and don't stress. My options are as follows: to use one of Mum's hugely expensive triple-gel razors (whatever "triple gel" means) and shave my whole scalp. Or beg Mum to write:

Dear Mrs Harding,
This is to inform you that Clover Jones will be unable to attend your wondrous educational establishment until her fringe has grown at least three centimetres. I know this may not be viewed as a valid

reason for absence, but believe me, the situation is desperate.

Yours sincerely,
Kerry Jones

P.S. Don't be too hard on Clover. It's all my fault for not letting her go to the Cutting Room.

As it's nearly July and hair grows at around a centimetre per month, this'll take until Christmas. Admittedly, my education will suffer, but at least by then I'll look less deranged.

"Clover!" Mum yells. "Stop sulking up there! Come on – I've got something to cheer you up."

Gritting my teeth, I grab my beanie hat, pull it down as low as it'll go and flump downstairs.

"What is it?" I ask, creeping into the kitchen.

"Look, darling," Mum says. "We made this for you." Her eyes gleam excitedly. I follow her gaze and peer at the cookie on a plate on the table. It's no ordinary cookie. It's so huge, it must have needed a whole baking tray all to itself. It's heart-shaped and covered with curly white icing patterns which have oozed into its craters. There's icing writing too. Splodgy letters which read: CLOVER WE LOVE U xxx.

It's the most beautiful cookie I've ever seen. Not

because it's all tidy like a bought cookie, but because they made it for me.

"I know it's late and everything," Mum says in a hoarse voice, "but I never got around to making you a birthday cake this year, did I? And I'm really sorry about the haircut and guitar lessons. . ."

"Thanks, Mum," I say in a jerky little voice.

She smiles at me, looking relieved. "Why are you wearing your hat, love?"

"Um, I'm cold," I mumble.

"You can't be," Mum insists. "It's so hot in here with the oven on. . ."

"Honestly, I just felt a bit chilly upstairs. . ."

"Oh, silly!" Mum giggles, snatching the beanie from my head and dropping her jaw in horror.

"Mum, I. . ."

She gawps at me as if I've sliced off my ear. "Oh my God," she whispers. "What have you done?"

I gulp, and try to focus on the cookie. "I . . . wanted a shorter fringe," I croak.

Mum hesitates, and her eyes moisten. "So you cut it yourself. . ."

I nod, ears burning. "Yeah."

"Oh, Clover, sweetheart," she says, wrapping her arms around me. "I can't believe you've done this to your beautiful hair. Why didn't you say?"

I *did* say, actually, but it feels so good being in Mum's arms, I don't want to bring up our row.

"It looks so funny," Lily chuckles. "Your forehead looks like a big plate!"

I choose to ignore this.

"Hey." Mum pulls away and squints at me. "We'll figure out something, OK?"

"Thanks," I mumble.

"Tell you what I'll do. I'll phone that new place – the Cutting Room, is it? – and I'll make you an appointment. They'll be able to fix it."

"Will you?" I gasp.

"Just this once, all right? I'm not doing this every time you need a trim. Honestly, Clover, you wouldn't believe how tight things are with money at the moment. . ."

"I won't go then," I say firmly. "I'll let Babs do it."

Mum shakes her head. "Look, I know how cut up you are about your guitar lessons, and I'm sorry you've had a rough time lately. . ." She tries for a smile, but it trembles, and I know she's thinking about Dad. "So I think you deserve a little treat," she adds quickly.

I swallow hard. It seems wrong now to spend so much on a haircut, but I can't imagine Babs being able to fix this mess. "Thanks, Mum," I say, snapping off the heart-cookie's point and popping it into my mouth. It melts on my tongue, sweet, buttery and delicious.

"And then," Mum adds eagerly, "I'll show you the lovely fur fabric I bought for our carnival costumes."

13

Fringe Correction

For the next few days, I keep a low profile. At least at the weekend I can keep my hat on all the time, and for school I manage to figure out a complicated system of clips to push my fringe to one side so it looks like I'm trying out a new style (sort of). I'm desperate to have it cut properly, but Mum couldn't get me an appointment until Friday – a whole eight days after my scissor disaster. Even Dad can hardly keep a straight face when he takes me and Lily out for lunch again (more Jurassic burgers – yum – but at least we haven't had to face meeting Bernice yet). I keep catching him glancing at my hair as if I'm wearing some kind of mad wig, but neither of us are allowed to mention it. I also call Niall, pretending to be ill, because I can't bring myself to tell him that we can't afford my lessons.

If all that's not enough to cause major stress, I'm also taking special care to avoid Riley as much as possible at school. For one thing, I still cringe every time I think about him coming round to our place when Mum was blasting her music. Another problem is that he's bound to mention my fringe. Every time he says hi and looks like he wants to chat, I scuttle away as if there's someone else I desperately need to talk to.

Friday rolls around at last. At lunchtime, having gobbled our canteen offerings at top speed, Jess and I head out to the park. Although it's a scorching hot day, I've got my beanie hat on which is making my scalp sweat like crazy. "Does Riley know you can't go to guitar lessons any more?" Jess asks as we perch on the low wall in the park.

"No," I tell her. "We haven't really spoken all week apart from a quick hi and stuff. After he heard Mum's music he probably thinks we're all crazy."

"Don't you think he might be a bit hurt?" she asks, frowning. "I mean, you invited him round, then didn't let him in, *and* you've been acting all weird around him ever since. . ."

"Yeah, I suppose so," I say glumly. "Anyway, there's no point practising guitar with him now, is there? He'll keep going to Niall and get better and better and he won't need to learn anything from me."

Jess smiles. "You think that's why Riley likes you? 'Cause you're so good at guitar?"

"Yeah, of course," I say firmly.

"You think that's *all* he likes?" She wiggles her

eyebrows, and even though she's my best friend, my ears flame up instantly.

"Yes!" I insist, laughing.

"Well, you know what you've got to do? Go and see Niall and explain what's happened, instead of this pretending-to-be-ill stuff, and see if he'll give you cheaper lessons or maybe not even charge you at all. . ."

"He won't do that," I scoff. "He's got a baby, it's his *job*. . ."

Jess looks exasperated. "You're his star pupil, aren't you? Surely he'll make an exception? It's got to be worth a try. . ."

"OK," I say, sighing. "What should I say?"

Jess throws open her arms. "*I* don't know! Tell him about your mum having no money and . . . hey, you're having your hair cut later, aren't you?"

"Yes, but. . ."

"So you're going to feel so good and confident," she charges on. "Why not go and see him straight afterwards?"

Sometimes, I wonder where I'd be without her. "OK, boss," I say with a grin.

By the time I've taken Lily home after school, then legged it back into town for my appointment, my bravado's all shrivelled up. Instead of marching right into the salon, I sidle past its glass door and walk on. I hope my casual expression says: "I'm *not* too freaked out to come in here – what gave you that idea? It's just that, before I make my grand entrance, I need to check out the buckets of rotting flowers outside Bloomin' Marvellous and the sad-looking unsold cakes in the bakery."

Having performed flower/cake duties, I creep back, my scalp itching beneath my beanie. The salon door flies open. Skelling's mother looms over me, newly high-lighted to match her darling daughter, frosted pink lips forming a scary grin. "Oh, Clover!" she gushes. "Are you coming in? Didn't know this was your kind of place!"

"Er, I come here all the time," I say firmly, transfixed by her mouth. Crystal goes to the same gym as Mum, although thankfully they're not especially friendly. Right now, her lipstick's so thick, it's a wonder it doesn't drip off and form a pink puddle on the pavement.

"Really?" she says, then adds, "I saw your mum in the Steak Shack last night. Looked like she was having a great time. . ." The gloopy lips form a smirk.

"It can't have been Mum," I say firmly. "She just went for a quick drink with a friend."

"Oh, it was definitely her," she insists, "looking very glam, all done up in a sparkly dress. Very short, it was. She's got the figure though, lucky thing. . ."

"Er, yeah," I mutter.

"Listen," she adds, dropping her voice to a whisper, "I know she's had a terrible time lately. So it was good to see her having fun with her, her . . . *friend*." She raises an over-plucked brow.

I fix her with a firm look, hoping it'll stop her from going on about Mum. OK, it's a bit weird that she didn't mention any restaurant last night. Maybe she felt guilty about spending money on steak. So she should, too. Aren't we supposed to be saving every penny?

Crystal smiles, engulfing me with her gag-making perfume. It's hard to believe this woman's an actual fashion designer. How the heck did she end up designing knickers for royalty? Do they phone her up personally every time they need a new order?

"I'd better go in," I say quickly, barging into the salon as Crystal swishes off down the street.

The receptionist scans the appointments book for my name. She has dark purple hair that's about five centimetres long all over. The salon smells of exotic fruit, and there's faint music that sounds like it's from somewhere like Brazil. I'm not used to this. I'm used to Babs lurching drunkenly for her hair gel.

"Oh, here you are," the receptionist says brightly, jabbing my name in the book. "Come over and we'll get you shampooed." She smiles kindly. "But better take your hat off first."

Reluctantly, I yank it off and stuff it into my bag. Another girl leads me to a basin. I'm draped with a rustling cape and swirled with suds that smell nothing like our blue hospitally stuff at home. Then I'm plonked in a chair in front of a vast mirror.

A woman with tumbling auburn waves drifts towards me. "Hi!" she says, combing out my damp hair. "What kind of thing d'you want today?"

She's a bit older than Mum – but then, everyone says Mum looks young, which gives me a warped view of other adults' ages. "I . . . I'm not sure," I say awkwardly. "You see. . ." I look down at my lap. "I cut my fringe myself. At least I tried to. . ." My jaw clenches.

Amazingly, the hairdresser doesn't laugh. She just smiles and says, "We've all done that, sweetheart. Reckon you got off lightly. But I'm going to suggest going much shorter to show off your lovely eyes and cheekbones . . . is that OK with you?"

I glance towards the receptionist. "Not *that* short," she adds quickly. "I'm thinking of soft layers to make the most of your gorgeous bone structure."

She glides away to grab some magazines from a table. I stare at my reflection, astounded. Gorgeous bone structure? I'd never realized I have one. Lovely eyes? Was she really talking to me? Then she's back, and we're flicking through magazines together, her honeyed voice washing over me like sunshine.

I hear myself agreeing to everything she suggests, and go all dreamy as she starts cutting. When Babs stabs at my hair, cackling with Mum, I'm usually a nervous wreck. Here I feel mellow and pampered.

"So what d'you like doing in your spare time?" she asks.

Normally, that'd sound like the kind of clunky old question adults come out with. But because she's so sweet and kind, I say, "Playing guitar, mostly."

"Really? When did you start?" she asks.

"When I was really little. About seven, I think."

"Gosh, that's young. . ."

"I had this uncle," I hear myself telling her. "Jupe, his name was. . ."

"That's an unusual name." She smiles at me in the mirror, encouraging me to go on.

"It was short for Jupiter. He was in a band. . ."

"Not *that* Jupe?" she gasps, holding her scissors mid-air.

"You knew him?" I ask.

"Of course I did! *Everyone* knew him. We had all his records at our house. . ."

"It's funny," I tell her. "You see, he was just Jupe to me. Well, not *just* Jupe. Me, my mum, dad and sister went for loads of holidays at his place in Cornwall when I was younger. It's probably all we could afford – I mean, we never went on proper abroad holidays – but I loved it anyway because I'd spend pretty much the whole time on the beach, or playing music with Jupe in his house. So," I add, realizing I've been babbling madly, "I almost forgot he was famous. Because he wasn't then, you see. It was sort of over for him."

She smiles. "They must have been brilliant holidays. . ."

I nod. "Yeah, they were."

"And didn't he. . ." She pauses, and her eyes meet mine in the mirror. "I'm sorry," she says quickly.

"Yes, he died. It was about a month ago now. How did you know?"

"Well," she says, flushing slightly, "there was quite a bit in the papers. Obituaries and things."

"Oh yes. Of course." Now I wish we hadn't started this conversation. She's nice and everything, but she's also a *stranger.* What was I thinking, telling her about Jupe? Apart from Jess, no one even knew about him at school. I was always worried that, if word got out, people would bring in embarrassing pictures of him that they'd printed off from the internet.

As if sensing my unease, the hairdresser starts cutting again. "Bet you're a good musician," she says, "if it's in the blood."

I shrug. "I know I can play. Writing songs is hard, though, because you want to sound like yourself and not like you're copying anyone else. . ."

"I'm sure you'll make it," she says. "There's something about you, I can tell."

I start to relax again as she finishes the cut, then nips off to the back room to fetch products. And it actually works. When she comes back and blow dries my hair, a new girl starts to emerge. Someone who might actually be someone one day. When I glance into the mirror, that's what I see: a new, improved Clover, with *bone structure.*

"Like it?" the hairdresser asks.

"Yes, I love it!" I enthuse. I look brighter all over. My skin's glowing and even my eyes are a more intense shade of green.

"I'm glad," she says, holding my gaze for a moment in the mirror. "I'm really glad, Clover."

It shocks me, the way she uses my name. Of course, it was in the appointments book along with everyone else's name. All those normal people who are allowed to come to proper hairdressers all the time instead of being held captive by drunk women with scissors. Even so, I wouldn't have thought a hairdresser in the poshest salon in town would have remembered *my* name.

I still feel floaty and weird as I hand over the money Mum gave me. Maybe it's the heady mixture of smells. It's too much – like scooshing yourself with all the perfume testers in the chemist's on a Saturday afternoon. How come, if Mum had to scrape the money together, she can afford to eat at the Steak Shack? Maybe she was out with a *man*, like Crystal Skelling was hinting, and he paid? So why didn't she tell me? It only feels like five minutes since Dad left. Surely she can't have met someone already?

"Oh, your hair's lovely!" the receptionist enthuses. "What a difference. You look great."

"Thanks," I say boldly.

"Hey, Bernice!" she calls across the salon. "That's a gorgeous cut you've done."

The hairdresser looks up, meets my gaze and blushes. My smile sets like cement.

Bernice?

My Crazed Stalker Episode

Copper Beach is probably *swarming* with Bernices. It can't be Nudie Bernice. I'm just overreacting because I'm in a posh salon and know I don't really belong here. The receptionist hands me my change. "Want a lift home tonight?" she calls to *fully clothed* Bernice.

Bernice shakes her head. "No, thanks. I'm, um . . . getting picked up."

"Is Geoffrey coming to get you?"

Something clamps my heart. This town's probably jam-packed with Geoffreys as well. My dad isn't the only one. There'll be loads of Bernices and Geoffreys who meet each other after work.

My eyes meet Bernice's. She looks blank and pale, as if someone's tried to rub her out.

Bernice-and-Geoffrey. It doesn't *mean* anything, I tell myself as I scuttle out, clutching a fistful of coins.

★

What a normal girl would do now is head straight over to Niall's and explain how things are with my family at the moment. "Sorry," Miss Normal would say, "but I can't come to guitar lessons any more. Mum says we can't afford it."

And Niall would smile and say, "Look, Miss Normal, I don't want you give up on yourself. I'm sure we can figure something out."

That's what Miss Normal would do. What I do is hurry down the street away from the Cutting Room, my ears sizzling, and lurk behind the gigantic plastic tubs outside Bloomin' Marvellous. The flowers' smells mingle, making me feel giddy. "Can I help you, dear?" An old lady in an overall has come out of the shop and is giving me a suspicious look.

"I, I'm just looking," I say quickly, pretending to study the wilting flowers.

"We're closing in a couple of minutes," she adds.

"Erm . . . I can't decide. I'll come back another time," I babble.

"Seeing as I'm packing up, you can have these carnations half price. . ."

"No, it's OK, thanks," I say, scarpering before she forces armfuls of shrivelled flowers on to me.

Further down the street, I peer into the newsagent's window at the adverts for old sofas and trampolines. Out of the corner of my eye, I see Bernice coming out of the hairdressers. She *can't* be Dad's girlfriend. Just had a minor freak-out there. No one would strip off and be an artist's model if they had a perfectly decent job as a hairdresser.

Another woman leaves the salon, then the receptionist. My breath feels thick and soupy in my throat.

Now a tall, slim man in pale jeans and a washed-out blue T-shirt is marching towards the salon. Seeing him, Bernice quickens her pace. He waves, and his face breaks into a grin. He tries to hug her, but she says something into his ear and quickly pulls away.

My heart turns cold. Dad's with that woman, in the street, in front of everyone. He takes her hand as they turn and quickly walk away.

My chest feels tight with anger. Did she realize it was me while she was cutting my hair? She must've done. She knew all about Jupe – there was hardly anything in the papers when he died – *and* she looked mortified when the receptionist said Geoffrey. I'm disgusted, and have an urge to muss up my haircut and spoil it. I almost want my botched fringe back.

And an awful thought flits into my head: *the money Mum had to scrape together for my haircut went straight to Nudie Bernice.* If she ever finds out, I'm dead.

I need to speak to Bernice – to ask why she let me sit there for half an hour with her hands all over my head. I mean, she could have *warned* me. I start to creep along after them. I can't help it.

They turn the corner, and I almost lose them among the crowd outside the Ship Inn. Early evening sunshine hits the pavement like a golden sheet. Once I'm through the crowd I spot them again, looking more relaxed now, chatting and giggling together.

They walk on, with her now gripping his arm, past Copper Beach Ices and the bandstand where I'll have to play the trombone now I'm destined to join a tragic old-man brass band. They pass the crumbling aquarium that's been shut down for years, and which Dad would never take me to anyway, as he refused to fork out for admission fees when we live by the sea. "Touristy rip-off," he always said. "Those places are a waste of the sun." He seemed to forget that the sun doesn't always shine on Copper Beach.

Dad and Bernice walk on, not noticing me darting along behind them, partly hidden by people strolling with ice creams on the seafront. They turn away from the sea and into a posh road where the front gardens have neatly trimmed hedges. Fury bubbles inside me. So this is where he lives. In a street – sorry, an *avenue* – where every house has a name like "The Lilacs" or "Briar Villa". Dad's gone posh. Some of the gardens have gnomes. If Dad's got one, I'm going to come back in the night and smash its stupid pointy hat off.

Then the houses become smaller. The street is really scruffy now, and some of the houses look like they'd crumble to bits if a bird landed on them. There are no gnomes. No one strolling with an ice cream. In fact there's hardly anyone here at all – just a drunk man shouting in a grocer's shop doorway – so I have to keep darting behind parked cars so Dad and Bernice don't spot me. My heart pounds frantically and my scalp prickles with sweat. Mum will be wondering where I am, and I can't even call her because she lost her mobile and asked to borrow mine. I'm the only person in my entire school who has to share a phone with her mum.

And the only one who stalks her own dad.

Face it, Clover – you're a sad, lunatic loser.

They stop, and I realize our car's parked there, outside my dad's new house, with its exhaust pipe dangling down. I stop too, frozen in shock. There's no car to hide behind. No bush to jump into. The whole world seems to fall silent as Dad stops in front of a scruffy green door and delves into his jeans pocket.

It's Bernice who turns first. She blinks at me and opens her mouth. Then she goes pale, like she did in the Cutting Room, and says something to Dad.

He looks round and squints and drops Bernice's hand. "Clover!" he gasps. "My God, what are *you* doing here?"

Dad's Love Nest (Shudder)

Excuses crash around my head.

I just happened to be walking this way.

I needed to talk to you about, er, something.

I'm not me. I'm a remarkably Clover-like android.

"Clover," Dad repeats, sounding concerned now, "what are you doing here? Did you follow us? Has something happened at home?"

I shake my head bleakly, wishing with every cell of my body that I'd gone straight home after my haircut. "I . . . she. . ." I nod at Bernice, who's now pulling a soppy, puppy-dog face. I wish she wouldn't. I don't want the pity of a nudie-model-cum-hairdresser person. "She . . . she cut my hair," I blurt out. "And then I realized, when I saw you coming to meet her. . ."

Dad's face softens, and he steps forward to enfold me in a hug. But I'm not in the mood for hugs. Not now, with Nudie gawping at us with her head tipped to one side, as if she's trying to mimic one of those oh-so caring agony aunts from Jess's magazines.

I wriggle away from him. "Did you know it was Clover?" he asks, turning to Bernice. "I mean, *my* Clover?"

For God's sake – how many weirdy-named Clovers are there are around here? "Of course I did," she says softly. "You've shown me so many pictures, darling. . ." *Darling. Agh. Puke.* ". . .And she's so pretty," Bernice warbles on, "with those striking green eyes and lovely cheekbones. . ." *Leave my cheekbones out of this.* ". . .The photos don't do you justice, Clover," she adds, fixing me with anxious blue eyes. "In fact, I started to think, no, she can't be . . . but then, when you mentioned your Uncle Jupe. . ."

"Why didn't you say it was you?" I blurt out, amazed that Dad took any family photos at all in that zip-up bag.

Bernice steps towards me. My instinct is to shrink away, but I stand firm, chin up, as if charged with super-powers. I feel different. Bolder, somehow. Maybe it's the haircut. Perhaps it *did* work, like Jess said it would. "It was hardly the right time," Bernice explains gently. "I didn't want to upset you or anything. . ."

"So what did you think," I demand, "when you realized it was me?"

"I . . . well, I was a bit panicked, so I nipped off to phone your dad, just to let him know you were there, but of course he didn't pick up the call. Men and mobile phones," she says with a small laugh. I don't laugh back. "But apart from that," she adds, "I just wanted to do the best haircut I could. And it wasn't easy, believe me, Clover. My hands were shaking the whole time. I'm amazed you didn't notice."

"Well, I didn't," I snap.

Dad smiles crookedly. "Well, sweetheart, now you're here, you'd better come in."

Oh hell. I hadn't considered this part. Why I've come here, and what I expect to happen next. I shuffle on the pavement as Dad unlocks the scruffy front door, and breathe in dust as I follow them up the dark, narrow staircase. I realize now that they don't live in *all* of this tiny house, but just the top half of it. It's a flat. A very, very small flat. Dad lets us in and we all stand uncomfortably in the minuscule hallway.

"Well," he says with an awkward cough, "this is our place, Clover. So, um . . . what do you think?"

I follow him into the living room. The "our", as in *our* place, jars my ears. "Nice view," I murmur, not knowing what else to say. I glance out through the grubby window at a dingy factory with a web of metal fire-escape stairs clinging to its wall. My hands are sweating. I'd give anything to be able to zap myself across town and be with Mum and Lily, scoffing cookies.

The only furniture in the room is a table, a very

new-looking stripy sofa and a wooden chest with a tiny TV plonked on it.

"Would you like tea, Clover?" Bernice flicks her eyes at Dad as if to say: *Is she old enough to drink tea?*

"Er, OK," I mutter.

"Sit down, sweetheart," Dad says, looking relieved as she scoots to the kitchen. "Tell me what's wrong. Why . . . why you followed us home."

He knows, of course. And I almost shout out, *Why d'you think? Because I was freaked out, OK? Which is quite understandable as your girlfriend had just cut my hair. . .*

"I . . . I just wanted to see you," I whisper, sitting awkwardly beside him.

"What about?" he asks gently.

"My guitar lessons," I blurt out, surprising myself. "Mum says I've got to stop going to Niall's because we can't afford my lessons any more." I look hopefully at Dad. Despite Jess egging me on today, the thought of pleading for free lessons from Niall is becoming more toe-curlingly embarrassing by the minute.

Dad frowns. "When did this happen?"

"About a week ago now. . ."

"Why didn't you tell me before?" he asks.

"I just . . . I thought I'd figure something out, or that Mum might even change her mind."

"Oh, Clover. It's not right that you should stop. I'll have a word with Mum, all right?"

"No, don't do that!" I cry. "She'll be mad that I told you. She doesn't even know I'm here. . ."

"The thing is," Dad adds, "I give your mum what I can afford. Honestly, Clover, I'm doing the best I can. So maybe she and I need to get together and have a little talk about how she can manage the money differently. . ."

"It's OK," I cut in, horrified at the prospect of Mum and Dad having a *little talk*. "I'm really not worried about my lessons. I was getting sick of them anyway."

"Come on, Clover. You *love* your guitar. . ."

"Yeah, but at this stage I'd probably get along better just learning by myself. I mean, I never had a teacher when I was little, did I?"

"Well. . ." Dad hesitates and looks me right in the eye. "You had Jupe, didn't you?"

I nod, not wanting to talk about Jupe right now, in case Bernice starts going on about how great he was when she didn't know him like we did. Dad looks relieved as Bernice emerges from the kitchen carrying two china cups (they might not have curtains but they do have saucers. Whoo, *posh*).

I take my tea from Bernice and sip it, scalding my top lip. There's a tense silence, then a tinkly noise as I rest my cup on its saucer. I flick my gaze around the room. Does Dad draw Bernice in here with her clothes off? Eek. Thankfully, she scurries back into the kitchen.

"Are you sure you're OK about stopping your guitar lessons, Clover?" Dad asks.

"Yes, honestly, Dad," I say firmly.

He nods, clearly not believing me. "You didn't really come here to talk about that, did you?" he asks, squeezing my hand.

I'm so jammed up inside, I don't know what to say. "I . . . just miss you," I manage to squeak out. "I . . . I know we still see you but it's not the same at home without you. I mean, we're doing OK, and Lily's all right, but I just feel so. . ." Tears spring into my eyes.

"Oh, darling." Dad holds my hand tightly, just as he'd held Bernice's in the street. "Look, I want you to know you can come here any time you like. . ."

"Of course you can," Bernice adds, appearing at the kitchen doorway. "I'd like to get to know you, Clover . . . if that's OK."

"All right," I mumble into my chest.

"And hopefully you'll bring Lily soon too," she adds, as if she knows the first thing about us.

I nod. "I'd better go now. Mum'll be getting worried."

Both of them see me downstairs to the street. "I'll drive you home," Dad says.

"I'd rather walk, Dad, honestly."

"OK, if you're sure." He hugs me and lowers his voice so Bernice can't hear. "Remember, love, you can call me any time. I'm. . ." He clears his throat, and I'm sure I spot a hint of wetness in his eyes. "I'm still here for you," he adds. "I'm still your dad."

"Yeah, I know that," I say, pulling away and hurrying home as fast as I can.

Mum's Mysterious Outing

The whole walk home, I try to get my head around Dad and Bernice living together in that titchy flat. Mum and Dad were never lovey-dovey or anything. But I'd never imagined Dad going off with anyone else and walking home with her hand-in-hand after work.

The first few days after Dad left, I kept telling myself he'd walk right back in at any minute. There'd be tears from Mum, and maybe more yelling, but at least they'd be back together again. Now I know that's not going to happen. It's way too late to stop off and see Niall, and I'm tired and hungry anyway. As I approach our street, I decide not to tell Mum about my little visit to Dad's new place, or that these days, he actually uses *saucers*.

Instead of Mum, though, I find Betty from next door plonked on our sofa with her crochet. "Hello, Clover," she says with a broad smile. "Good day at school?"

"Er, yes, thanks, Betty. Um, isn't Mum home?"

"She's gone out," Betty explains. "With you having your hair done after school – it looks lovely, dear – she asked if I'd pop in to look after Lily." She pauses and furrows her forehead at me. "How are . . . *things*, Clover?"

Lily is sprawled belly-down on the living room floor surrounded by glittery glue pens and paper. "Um, everything's fine," I say quickly. Her look says: *Oh, pity the poor urchin waif.*

"It's just, if you ever. . ." she begins.

"D'you know where Mum's gone?" I cut in.

"She didn't say. Probably her aerobics class. Does she still go to the gym? Not that she needs to, she's looking terribly thin. . ."

Lily flicks her eyes up at me. "Mum didn't go to aerobics," she announces. "She was really dressed up with shiny high heels and a new dress that was kind of animally. . ."

"Animally?" I repeat.

"Yeah," she says, eyes popping. "Like, like . . . a *leopard*."

A leopard dress? To the gym? "When did she say she'd be home?" I ask Betty.

"She didn't," Betty replies. "She just popped round and asked me to stay with Lily until you came back. That's all she said. . ."

This is weird. I feel odd the whole time Betty chatters on about whether she should get a new cat to replace Midnight, and odder still when she's gone home and it's just Lily and me. It's half-eight – past Lily's bedtime. She's lounging on the sofa watching *Dumbo*. It's far too babyish for her, and I start to worry that her mental development has skidded into reverse and that soon she'll ask for her old dummy back.

I fetch my guitar and start strumming beside her, despite the fact that it's still missing a string. "Can't hear the film," Lily protests.

"You should be upstairs in bed by now," I tell her. "Why are you watching *Dumbo* anyway?"

She glowers at me. "Stop telling me what to do. When's Mum coming back?"

"Soon," I say irritably. How should I know? I don't even know where she is! You don't wear a leopard dress and high heels to aerobics. No, she's gone *out* out. To a pub or the Steak Shack, maybe with a man, despite being bankrupted by my haircut and Dad only leaving about *six seconds ago*.

The doorbell rings, and I fling my guitar on to the sofa and rush to answer it.

Riley's standing there, dampened by drizzle. "Hi!" I say, my heart leaping.

"Er, can I come in?" he says. "I, um, like your hair, by the way. . ."

"Oh, do you?" My cheeks surge pink. "Um, yeah, course you can," I add, leading him into the kitchen. He glances around awkwardly. I wonder if I should explain why Lily's still up and watching *Dumbo*, but decide it's far too complicated.

"I . . . I just wanted to ask you. . ." he begins.

"Ask me what?" I say, trying to seem casual and normal.

"I just wondered. . ." He pauses. Cartoony music filters through from the living room. "Um, is something wrong, Clover?" he asks. "I mean, did I do something to upset you?"

"No," I say quickly. "I—"

"'Cause since I came over," he cuts in, "and Lily answered the door and said you'd gone out to look for your dog. . ."

"Uh-huh. . ." I say, my ears sizzling as if they've been dunked into Tony's deep fryer.

". . .You've hardly spoken to me," he adds.

"Well," I bluster, "I'd had this hair disaster and I was just trying to keep out of everyone's way. . ."

Riley gives me a *you-are-crazy* look. "It wasn't just that, though, was it? I mean, you've said hi and stuff when you really had to, but more often you've gone out of your way to avoid me. . ."

I look down, wishing I could slip down a crack in the floor. "I just felt a bit . . . embarrassed, that's all," I murmur. The house feels too still and hushed as I glance back up at Riley. Even *Dumbo*'s gone quiet.

"What about?"

"That . . . that day you came round," I say, clearing

my throat. "It was a bad time. Mum has these . . . these *things* sometimes, when she plays her music really loud and doesn't care about it blaring into the street or anything—"

"So you were in the whole time?" Riley gives me an incredulous look.

"Yeah," I mutter.

"And you thought I wouldn't want to come in when your mum was playing that stuff."

I nod wordlessly. "God, Clover, d'you think I don't know about embarrassing parents? Never met my dad, have you?"

"No. . ."

"Never seen him in his hairy old sweaters and tie-dyed trousers?"

I splutter as the grin spreads across my face. "Honestly? Your dad wears tie-dye?"

"Does it himself," Riley says, smirking. "T-shirts, trousers, even my bedroom curtains once – anything he can get his hands on. He had a market stall before we moved here, but I guess the demand for tie-dye dried up. He ended up having to get a boring old office job doing filing instead. What he'd really like to be is a musician, but three chords are about his limit. . ."

"So," I say, "did your dad get you into playing guitar?"

"Yeah. And he's too kind to say I'm rubbish."

"But you're not—" I try to argue.

Riley smirks. "It's OK, Clover. I can take it, y'know. I see how stressed Niall gets, dealing with me, holding up the whole class. . ."

I can't help smiling, because it's true.

"How about you?" he asks. "What made you start playing?"

A scene flashes into my mind. Jupe in Crickle Cottage. Me on the old, bashed-up sofa, being handed a guitar that felt almost as big as me. And Jupe saying, "Just strum it, Clover, like this." We'd all planned to go to the beach that day, and Mum, Dad and my toddler sister were all waiting, laden with plastic buckets and spades.

"I don't want to go," I announced, to their amazement. "I want to play guitar with Jupe."

"Clover?" Riley's voice jolts me back to reality.

"Oh, it was my uncle," I say quickly. "He was in a band years and years ago. I suppose he got me started."

"Was he famous?" Riley asks.

I look up at him. I could say no, and that would be that – conversation over, neatly folded away. "Yeah," I say, "kind of."

"Is that why you're so good? 'Cause he's still teaching you?"

"No, um, he died a few weeks ago. . ."

"Oh, I'm sorry." Riley's hazel eyes meet mine.

"It's OK," I say, shrugging. "I hadn't seen him for

years. We had . . . a sort of family falling out and Mum never spoke to her own big brother again."

"Really? Was it that bad?"

I shrug. "Yeah. I've never understood why they didn't try to patch things up. . ."

"God," Riley breathes. "So was he, like, really famous? Would I know him?"

I hesitate, because I'm so used to keeping the Jupe thing pretty secret. But something about Riley makes me think he won't laugh about my mad uncle, or spread it around school. It's so much nicer being with him here, just the two of us, instead of having Skelling forever hanging around, shooting me snidey looks. "Well, he used to tour the world with his band," I explain, "and he wore these . . . gold leather trousers." I pause, waiting for him to splutter or something, but he doesn't. He just keeps looking at me. "And ages ago," I continue, "way before I was born, he was on the cover of every music magazine. . ."

"Wow," Riley says, eyes wide. "So who was he?"

I sense myself blushing slightly. "He was in a band called Falcon. . ."

Riley frowns. "D'you have any pictures?"

"Yeah, just one."

I take him upstairs to my room and show him a crinkly old picture I keep under my socks in my drawer. It's been cut out of a magazine. You can tell it's really old because on the other side is an advert for make-up and it looks really old-fashioned.

Riley studies the photo. Jupe's wearing a terrible scarlet blouse with ruffles all down the front. *Now* I expect him to laugh, or say something rude about the blouse, but he doesn't.

"I know who he is!" he exclaims. "My dad likes him. He's got some of his records, used to play them when I was younger before our old turntable broke. . ."

I study the photo over Riley's shoulder. I've only ever shown Jess this picture. She laughed when I told her that he'd named himself after a planet – Jupiter – because Uranus wouldn't have looked good on posters. But she didn't get his music, and why should she? She didn't *know* him.

"Riley," I say hesitantly, "I can't come to lessons at Niall's any more."

He pushes back his fringe and places the photo on the cluttered dressing table. "I know. Jess told me what happened with your mum. Listen, we're going to fix something, OK? I called Niall and told him. He wants you to go round and see him, soon as you can."

Dumbo's credits are rolling and I hear Lily bounding upstairs. "Hello, Riley," she says shyly, poking her head around our bedroom door.

"Hi, Lily. Good movie?"

She nods, and I detect a hint of embarrassment over her viewing choice. "Bed for you," I announce as the front door bangs open.

Ah. Mother returns. I step out on to the landing with Riley beside me, my stomach swirling anxiously. "Mum?" I call down.

"Sorry I'm late, honey," she cries. "Oh, hello . . . um, Riley, isn't it?" She peers up at us, looking a little unsteady on her feet.

"Yeah, hi," he says, heading casually downstairs as if all of this is completely ordinary.

Mum tries, unsuccessfully, to smooth down her hair. "Had a few drinks with a friend," she explains with a giggle. "Hey, they've done a great job at that Cutting Room, don't you think, Riley?"

I glare at her. She *is* drunk. I can smell it on her as I head downstairs. How does she manage to squeeze maximum embarrassment out of any situation? *How?*

"Pretty thing, isn't she?" Mum adds teasingly.

I try to figure out how to liquefy myself so I can sink into our carpet, like a stain.

Riley nods and mumbles something I don't catch. He's snatched his jacket from the chair in the hall and is speedily pulling it on. Desperate to escape from Lunatic Mansions, I guess.

"Maybe I should get myself down there," Mum babbles on, her words melting into each other, "and have the same person cut mine. Time for a new image, I reckon – what d'you think, Clover?"

I shrug and look away. Riley flicks me a quick

glance. Compared to Mum's performance, having a parent tie-dye your curtains counts for *nothing.*

"Can't remember who it was," I say quickly.

"Oh, come on. You *must* remember." Mum giggles idiotically.

"It was Janice, I think, or maybe Jenny. . ."

"Well, we'll have to find out, won't we?" Mum says. "Maybe you were right, love. I've been seeing Babs for years and sometimes you can fall into a rut with the same old hairdresser. . ."

"Mum, come upstairs and see me!" Lily demands from our room. Thank you, little sister. Quickly, I open the front door and step out with Riley, breathing in a lungful of cool air.

I look at him. "Sorry," I say lamely.

He smiles. "Don't be. It's fine."

There's a moment of stillness and then, far away, the squawk of a gull. "Can I come over again?" he asks.

"Sure you want to?"

"Course, why wouldn't I?"

I smile. "Yeah, that'd be good." I don't ask about Skelling and whether she's his girlfriend or whatever, because right now, it doesn't seem to matter.

Even Mum being drunk in that leopardy dress doesn't matter.

Nothing does. Because, as Riley lifts a hand to my face, right now is all that matters. Gently, looking at me the whole time, he pushes away a strand of hair. There's a pause, and I think I'm holding my breath. Then his lips are on mine, soft and sweet.

And I am really kissing Riley Hart.

For ages and ages.

I think I'm going to explode or faint. Then I feel myself dissolving, like that heart-shaped cookie, melting away to nothing.

We stop, and every cell in my body is tingling madly as I say, "Riley . . . we don't have a dog."

When your heart's about to explode into billions of sparks, a little white lie doesn't matter. He doesn't care about Bambi, our fictitious dog. He just looks at me and turns a bit pink, then murmurs, "I, um . . . I like you, Clover."

I like you, Clover! I know he's hardly declared undying love or anything. But still. He likes me. He likes me! And I don't know whether to tell him I like him too, or to say, "That's nice" or something equally feeble. I'm completely awestruck. Maybe that's why I start babbling, "Well, if we did have a dog, and I wish we did, I wouldn't call him Bambi. I'd call him, er, Brian or something."

"Brian?" Riley repeats, raising an eyebrow.

"Well, you know, as a joke . . . ha ha. . ."

"Yeah," he says, looking confused, "Brian's *so* much better than Bambi. . ."

"No, I didn't mean. . ." *Stop it, Clover! Stick a sock in*

it. Riley looks at me. Then we shuffle a bit, and I can't risk saying anything else in case I blurt out more ridiculous dogs' names. Which kind of kills the romantic moment.

"So, er, see you at the weekend maybe?" he asks.

"Uh-huh," I croak.

"Great. Bye then, Clover."

As he mooches off down our street, I stand at our front door for a moment, hanging on to his words. *I like you, Clover.*

"I like you too," I whisper, my heart pounding madly as he disappears from view.

By the time I'm back in the living room, I've started to wonder if I actually imagined Riley saying those words or even kissing me. Can the human brain actually do that – make you think you've kissed someone when it's just your mind playing a terrible trick? I touch my lips with my fingertips. They certainly *feel* kissed – kind of warm and tingly. Trust me to spoil the moment by going on about dogs.

I glance over at Mum, who's watching me sleepily from her curled-up position on the sofa. "So, you had a boy in your bedroom?" she asks with a frown.

"He's just a friend, Mum," I say quickly.

"I know he is . . . but be careful, darling. . ."

"Mum, it's nothing! We were just chatting and stuff."

She nods, meeting my gaze. "Well, I hope so."

I turn away, wanting to curl up in bed and replay that

thing Riley said over and over until I'm asleep. *I like you, Clover. . .*

"Goodnight, Mum," I say.

"Goodnight, sweetheart." Before I've even left the room, Mum's fallen asleep in her leopardy dress and red patent heels, a crazy smile on her face.

17

Lily in the Middle

Next morning, there's no mention of Mum's mystery night out, although I detect that she's squirted herself with a new perfume called Hint of Guilt. She flaps around us, cooking our usual Saturday fried breakfast. Although I probably should be annoyed with her, I'm in too good a mood after my kiss with Riley (which I've decided definitely *did* happen). Anyway, maybe Mum was just out with a friend, trying to chat up men or something. I can't believe she'd do that when it still feels as if Dad's only just gone. But it's better, I suppose, than her feeling all bitter and angry. I just hope Mum remembers she has me and Lily and doesn't need anyone else.

Later on, when I've wondered about eight hundred times whether to call Riley just to say hi, he phones *me* on my mobile (thank God I managed to get it back from Mum). "Just wondered," he says, "if I can come over with my guitar?"

"Yeah, sure," I say, trying to sound as if it's completely normal to hang out with a boy at the weekend.

Five things I do before he arrives:

1. Carry out thorough check for embarrassing items left on bedroom floor (knickers, bras, scraps of paper on which I'd been absent-mindedly merging my name with his – *Clover Hart.* The cringe-making shame of it).
2. Pay Lily two pounds to clear off.
3. Breathe heavily and pace around a lot.
4. Explain to Mum that my, uh, *friend* Riley's coming over in about an hour and will it be OK for us to play music in my room? I.e., could she please *not* put on her own CDs full blast? "Of course I won't," she says. "You only have to say, darling." As if it's usually that simple.
5. Call Jess to tell her about last night's kiss, and the fact that Riley's due at my house in approximately forty-five minutes and sixteen seconds.

"Does this mean he's your boyfriend now?" she yelps.

"I don't know," I tell her.

"Well, are you going to ask him?"

"Of course not!" I shriek, my stomach swirling with panic. How is *anyone* supposed to know what to do in this kind of situation? It's not as if I'd ever even kissed a boy until last night. The thought of more kissing, in my bedroom with Mum likely to burst in at any moment, almost makes me want to call Riley back and tell him not to come.

I manage not to do that, and in fact, apart from both of us acting a bit shy and awkward when he shows up, it's actually not stressful at all. "Sorry about Mum last night," I say as we try those bar chords again.

"Your mum's fine," Riley says with a grin. "She probably just wanted to go out and have a good time."

"Yeah, I guess you're right. I'm just not used to it. . ."

"What, your mum having a good time?" he laughs.

I nod and my face breaks into a smile.

"Are you good at guitar, Riley?" Lily blurts out from the doorway.

"Lily," I hiss, throwing a stern look at her.

"It's OK," Riley says. "C'mon in, Lily. No, I'm not very good, but Clover's helping me get better – I *hope*. . ."

"Can you show me?" she asks, stepping into our room, obviously forgetting that I paid her two quid to stay out.

"Yeah, sure," Riley says. Now, this isn't what I'd imagined at all: the three of us here, with Riley patiently showing Lily how to make an A-chord shape.

"Clover never shows me," she retorts. "She won't even let me *touch* her guitar."

"Big sisters can be so mean," he chuckles.

"Oh, right," I retort. "Like all the times I've taken

you swimming, and sat drawing with you, and spent all my money on Cedric's tunnel. . ."

"She's all right really," Lily chips in with a grin, and my heart softens a little. Sometimes my little sister can be almost . . . sweet.

In fact, weirdly enough, I start to feel *pleased* that she's here with us. While Lily's in the room, there's no chance of any more kissing, which means I'm not stressing out about it either happening or *not* happening, or Mum walking in and catching us and making a huge fuss. The next couple of hours fly by, and as Riley gets ready to leave, I don't even feel like asking Lily for my two quid back.

"So you'll speak to Niall about your lessons?" Riley asks at the front door.

"Yep, I'll definitely do that."

"It'll be fine," he says, turning to go. "See you Monday, OK?"

"Yeah, see you at school. . ." I pause, wondering if I should just say it: *D'you want to go out sometime?* Riley stops too, as if he can read my mind, and knows I'm trying to pluck up the courage.

"Bye, Riley!" Lily trills, skipping downstairs from our room and stopping all breathless at the front door. "Thanks for the guitar tips!"

The grin warms his face, and those hazel eyes sparkle in the pale afternoon sun. "Any time," he replies, before nodding his goodbye and striding off down the street.

I turn and step back inside. "He's nice," Lily blurts out.

I nod. "Yeah, he is."

"So are you his girlfriend now?"

"Er, not really, Lil. . ."

"Why not?" she wants to know. What can I say? *Because how could anything happen with you hanging out with us for most of the afternoon?* I don't even mind – not really. Seeing him helping Lily to play his guitar showed another side of Riley – an even nicer side. As if there wasn't enough to like already. "Why aren't you his girlfriend?" she asks again, furrowing her pale brow. "He likes you, Clover. I can tell he does."

"Oh, Lily," I laugh, sensing my cheeks turning pink. "I can't explain it. You're just too young to understand, OK?"

I head over to Niall's on Sunday morning straight after breakfast. "What I was thinking," I say as he beckons me in, "is that I could do a bit of babysitting . . . er, maybe in exchange for a lesson. . ." I swallow hard, wondering if that sounded horribly cheeky.

"You're pretty young to babysit," he says with a smile.

"Yeah, I know, but I helped loads with Lily when she was little. I played with her and read her stories and stuff."

"How old were you then?" he asks.

"Um, five or six." Suddenly, I feel silly. It sounds too young to be useful, although it really felt like I was.

When she was crying I'd hold her close, and within seconds she'd be smiling her toothless smile.

"Early starter," Niall says with a chuckle. "Look, Clover, I heard you were going through a pretty tough time at home. I was going to call you and say, if it's OK with your mum, we can forget paying for lessons for a while. I mean, it's a group lesson and you'll be helping me really, because you're great at showing the others what to do. . ."

"Not last time, I wasn't," I say quickly.

"Well, you are usually, and I'm happy with that arrangement if you are. . ."

"I can't *not* pay, Niall! I'd feel bad. Maybe, if I could help with the baby, then it'd seem fairer. . ."

He pauses for a moment. "OK. You're probably a bit young to babysit in the evenings, but maybe you could do a couple of hours after school – say once a week – so Jen could go for a swim or something? I'd only be upstairs in the workshop if you needed me. What d'you say?"

"I'd love to do that," I enthuse.

"And in return you can have lessons, *and* you don't have to feel bad. OK?"

"OK," I say, fizzling with delight. "I'll just have to check with Mum."

I come home to find Mum and Lily surrounded by swathes of brown fur fabric, chatting excitedly. "What's this for?" I ask.

"We're going to be the three bears!" Lily exclaims.

"And you, Clover," Mum announces, "will be Mummy Bear." I blink at her, confused. "The carnival, remember?" she says, laughing.

"Oh, Mum . . . do I have to be in it this year? Shouldn't *you* be Mummy Bear?"

"No, love," she says briskly. "I'm the biggest, so I'm Daddy, and you're middle-sized so you're Mummy. . ."

"But me and Lily are getting far too old for it, and—"

"I'm not too old," Lily declares. "I can't *wait* for the carnival."

"Don't be such a spoilsport, Clover," Mum laughs. "Anyway, it's only a week away now so we need to get organized. What d'you think of our costume idea?"

What do I *think*? That this is hardly how I planned to present myself in public shortly after my thirteenth birthday. But, heck, after my chat with Niall I'm in too good a mood to protest. "OK, I suppose I'll do it." *As if I have any choice.*

"And I'm Baby," Lily exclaims, struggling into her costume. The head part has an oval-shaped hole for her delighted face to peep through. "Like it?"

"You look great," I manage.

Mum perches on the living room table, which is piled high with her sewing things. "Look, love," she says, "I know you don't really want to do this, but it'll be nice to do something together, the three of us. . ."

"It's all right, Mum," I say. "I don't mind, honestly. But, um . . . can I ask you something?"

"Uh-huh."

"Is it OK if I look after Niall's baby for a couple of hours a week?"

Her forehead crinkles. "You're too young to look after a baby, Clover. . ."

"Yes, but Niall would be at home too, upstairs in his workshop where he fixes guitars. So I wouldn't really be on my own. I'd just be helping out so Jen could have a break. . ."

"Mm-hm," Mum says warily.

"And in return Niall says he'll give me free lessons," I finish all in a rush.

"Can I help with the baby too?" Lily demands.

"No, sorry. . ."

"Please, I love babies!"

Mum looks at her. "Listen, hon, that's sweet of you, but Clover needs to do this on her own, right?"

"That's right, Mum."

"Well, I don't see any harm in it. And I'm proud of you for sorting this out instead of moaning at me."

I grin, and I'm glowing all over as if Riley just kissed me again, right here in front of my mum and sister and piles of fur fabric. Mum holds up an almost-finished outfit. "This is for you."

"It's great!" I say with fake enthusiasm.

"Oh, and listen, girls," Mum adds hesitantly, "on

Saturday, after the carnival, I've got, um, a little surprise for you."

"What is it?" Lily and I cry in unison.

Although Mum looks a little uneasy, there's no hiding the excitement in her eyes. "Just . . . something I want to tell you about. You'll see."

Something Goes Right

I don't have time to ponder Mum's surprise because the whole week's taken over by carnival fever. "Not long to go now," Skelling cackles, trailing behind me along the corridor towards science. "Hope you've got your costume ready, Clover. Can't wait to see it, can we?" There's an outburst of giggles. I'm determined not to look round. "Gone deaf, have you?" she calls out. I'm aware of her clopping along behind me, her footsteps growing closer until she catches up with me at the classroom door. Three of her friends hang back, smirking, as if eager to see what happens next.

"It's none of your business what I'm doing for the carnival," I snap.

"Oh." Her pencilled eyebrows shoot upwards. "So you won't be coming down to the beach after the parade with me and Riley and the others?" She affects a wide-eyed, innocent face which I could happily slap.

"I don't know what I'm doing," I say coolly, striding into the science lab.

All afternoon, I ponder what to do after the parade on Saturday. There's no reason why I *shouldn't* hang out with Riley, even if Skelling's there too. I know, though, that she'll make me feel like a gatecrasher. I feel tense already, and there are still five days to go. Plus, I have the bear costume horror to deal with, too. I can picture it now: Skelling wearing some teeny dress the size of a hankie. And me, decked out in top-to-toe brown fake fur. Riley hurries into class, five minutes late, and is given a sharp telling off by Mr Featherstone. I keep my gaze firmly fixed upon the cross sections of leaves in my textbook.

I'd been hoping that Riley and I would walk down to Niall's together after school, but when the bell goes I spot him chatting animatedly to Skelling, who's still wearing her navy shorts and polo shirt after gym. "Hi, Clover," she says, all smiles.

"Hi, Sophie."

"How are you getting on with guitar these days?"

"Er, fine. . ." I glance at Riley. He swings his guitar as the three of us head away from school.

"Riley's getting much better," Skelling adds, turning to him. "That time you were round at mine and played those songs . . . God, they were so good, like really professional. . ."

"I don't think so, Sophie," he splutters.

She rolls her eyes. "He could be a pop star, don't you think?"

"Um, maybe," I mumble, quickening my pace until we reach Skelling's road and she peels, reluctantly, away from us.

"Enjoy your lesson, you two," she trills after us.

"Thanks, Soph," he calls back.

Riley and I fall into silence as we walk on. What did she mean, he's been over at hers, playing songs for her? My stomach twists with envy. *Get a grip*, I tell myself as we amble along the tree-lined road towards Niall's. *You've had one kiss. He comes over to play guitar at your house. It's nothing, OK? Well, not nothing exactly. You're just friends and he's obviously friends with her too. It's no big deal. . .*

"Clover?" Riley stops and looks at me. "You're not listening, are you? You're miles away."

"What? Oh, sorry. . ."

"I was just asking if you're going to be in the parade on Saturday."

"Oh!" I exclaim. "Erm, maybe. I'll see. I haven't decided yet." What made me say that? I could hardly sleep for Mum's sewing machine buzzing away like an insect last night.

Niall's dug out some tricky finger-picking exercises for us this week. Having to concentrate hard takes my mind off Skelling and the carnival and all the other stuff that's been clogging up my mind too much lately.

"That was fantastic, Clover," Niall says after the lesson. I sense Riley glancing at me in admiration. That's what I like about him (just one of the hundreds of things I like about him). The way he's not hung up on being the best.

"Thanks," I say, beaming.

"You really should take this further, you know," Niall adds as we all get ready to leave. "You write songs, don't you?"

"Well, I try," I say. "The problem is, I can't sing."

"Oh, I bet you can. . ."

I laugh. "Honestly. Last time I tried, our hamster wouldn't come out of his tunnel."

"Well," Niall chuckles, "maybe you don't *have* to sing. You could find someone who can. What about you, Riley? I've heard you. There's a good voice in there, trying to come out. . ."

Riley blushes furiously. "Don't think so, Niall. . ."

He shrugs. "You should work on it, you know. Build your confidence. And Clover, there are people are out there who want to play the music you do. They might just take some squirrelling out."

"Maybe," I say, wondering where on earth I'd start squirrelling at Horsedung.

"What did you think of that?" Riley asks as we leave Niall's together and step out into the warm afternoon.

"What, about starting a band? I'd love to, but. . ."

"But what?" he asks.

"Um, I've never really played with anyone else. Only my uncle, really. . ."

"And me," he says with a smile.

"Yeah, but. . ."

"You don't want *me* in your band," he teases, and my cheeks flush pink.

"It's not that," I insist. "It's just . . . it seems like such a huge thing – finding people, somewhere to rehearse, and I can imagine what Mum'd make of us all crammed into my bedroom, making a racket. Then Lily'd be popping in every two minutes, begging to join in. . ."

"How did your uncle get started?" he asks as we reach the end of his street.

I pause. "With school friends, I think."

"Well, there you go. . ."

"But it was different for him," I add, remembering the promise I made to Jupe in that letter: *To make up for everything, the only thing I can think of is to be the best guitarist I can possibly be and start a band and be amazing.*

"Well," Riley says carefully, "maybe you should believe in yourself more."

I look at him, at those hazel eyes which are dappled with sunshine. "You're right," I say, smiling. "Maybe I should."

19

Carnival Fever

Every spare minute over the next few days, I hide away in my bedroom and practise Niall's finger-picking exercises. Not that I have huge amounts of extra time: on Wednesday, straight after school, Mum sends me straight over to Betty's next door to help to make the customary bunting to decorate her house for carnival day. Betty has trunks stuffed with fabric, and it's quite soothing, rummaging through it all and picking out pieces that'll go together. She then has me cutting out triangles, which she hems on her sewing machine.

"How's things these days, Clover?" she asks, delving into a basket to find lengths of tape long enough for the bunting.

"OK," I say lightly.

"Still playing your music?"

"Oh yes. . ."

"That nice friend of yours has been to see you again, hasn't he? The one who brings his guitar. . ."

I smile and glance over at Betty. "You mean Riley?"

She nods, and her eyes glint mischievously. "Hmm. The good-looking one."

"Yes, but he's just a friend, Betty," I say with a grin.

"That's good, Clover. Looks like a nice boy. So, been seeing much of your dad lately?"

"Er. . ." I pause, wishing she hadn't brought him up. Dad's invited me and Lily over after school tomorrow. The thought of sitting there balancing china teacups on saucers, with Bernice going on about my bone structure. . . "We speak quite a lot," I say lightly, "and I'm seeing him tomorrow."

Betty nods, and I catch her giving me the occasional glance as the sewing machine whirrs back into life. "This is looking great," she exclaims, holding up one end of a finished strip of bunting. "Here, you take the other end and let's have a look."

Obediently, I take the other end of the tape and step back until it's stretched taut, stepping carefully over Midnight's food bowl, which still sits by the door, even though he died months ago now.

"Well, that's that piece done," Betty says brightly. "Could you bear to cut out more triangles for me or had you better get home?"

I pause, thinking of my bear costume lying on our kitchen table, ready for me to try on for the fiftieth time. "Just a few more alterations," Mum had said earlier.

"Oh, I think I'll stay here and cut triangles," I say with a grin.

Tea at Dad and Bernice's next day isn't too bad, especially as Bernice has baked specially for us – the table is laden with cupcakes – and we're allowed Coke, which Mum hardly ever buys. "I think I'm gonna be a hairdresser," Lily announces as Bernice styles my sister's thick, dark hair into a sophisticated updo. I can tell Bernice is trying to be especially nice to Lily, who's lapping up all the attention.

"You'll probably change your mind a million times before then," Dad says with a smile.

"What do you want to be, Clover?" Bernice asks as we clear the table together.

I'm about to remind her of my music thing, but feel less comfortable sharing my hopes and plans than I did at the Cutting Room. "Haven't decided yet," I say lightly.

What I have decided, though, is that there's no way Lily can show up at home with her hair piled up professionally like that. On the way home, just around the corner from Dad's, we stop so I can pull out all the clips.

"I don't want to take it all out!" Lily protests, cheeks flaming angrily.

"You'll have to," I say firmly.

"But why? I wanna show Mum!" Her bottom lip trembles and her eyes flood with tears.

"Look, I'm sorry. . ." I stuff the clips into my jacket pocket and try to smooth down her hair. "It's just . . . Mum'll be upset if she sees it, Lil."

"Why?" she cries.

"Because Bernice did it."

"So what? It's my hair! It's nothing to do with Mum!"

"Listen," I say firmly, "I've got all the clips, OK? I watched how she did it and sometime I'll put it up for you exactly the same."

Her lip curls and she gives me a suspicious look. "You're rubbish at hair. You made your fringe all up-and-downy."

I grab her hand and start walking briskly. "Yeah, well, that was cutting," I say. "Putting it up's a lot easier. You can help me – we'll play hairdressers sometime." That perks Lily up. My other hand curls around the clips in my pocket, and I wonder how something as simple as hair suddenly got so complicated.

All of Friday, I try to think about anything but the carnival. Maybe it'll be called off. Perhaps, if I wish hard enough, there'll be a freak hurricane. Then it'd be unsafe to have the parade with all those floats with people dancing on them. It doesn't sound right, almost wishing a natural disaster would happen. But that's how desperate I am.

20

Fuzzy Bear Horrors

Before I've opened my eyes next morning, I can feel sunshine beating hard on my face. Great. Carnival Day looks set to be the hottest day of the year. Just what you need when you're bundled up in fur fabric. I find Mum and Lily downstairs, giggling together as they struggle into their costumes. "Couldn't we put them on in town, just before the procession starts?" I suggest.

"No," Mum says firmly. "Everyone arrives in their costumes, Clover. Anyway, Betty will be dying to see you all dressed up." Maximum humiliation, she means. So I moan a bit more, then climb into my rug suit and we set off – Daddy, Mummy and Baby Bear – but not before our photocall with Betty. "Just one more!" she trills, waggling her old-fashioned camera at us. I blink through the eyeholes of my costume. *It's only one day*, I remind myself. *One day, then everything will be normal again.*

By the time we've plodded into town, my whole body's slithering in sweat. The streets are thronging with cavemen, hula dancers and every cartoon character imaginable. There's even a giant papier mâché Dumbo. I spot Skelling, who's come as a glammed-up version of herself in a tiny white dress and silver sandals. Inside my fat furry costume, my flesh crawls.

At the front of the assembled parade, an old-man band starts parping. We start plodding behind the hula girls. I feel slightly sick as the bass drum thumps in time with my pounding heart.

Skelling is posing on the pavement, and bursts into giggles when she spots my furry family. I try to send hostile vibes through my eyeholes. No sign of Riley yet. Maybe he'll miss the whole spectacle and I can tell him about it and miss out the embarrassing bits (which, come to think of it, means *all* of it).

As the procession stomps on, I remember Mum mentioning a little surprise a few days ago – something she wanted me and Lily to see on Carnival Day. What'll it be? Maybe dinner at the Steak Shack? She does a wiggly dance for the crowd, who send out a cheer. The hula dancers shake their raffia skirts; then they part and, through the gap, I spot an older man in a long brown coat with matted fur around its hem. He's dancing, if you could call it that – kind of jiggling his arms and swaying his hips and making his long hair fly about. Walking beside him is a thinner, slightly shorter figure, also in an ancient hippie coat with long black hair bushing down his back.

I focus hard on the hippies.

"Oh look!" Lily squeals as the boy turns round. "Look at those men in the long coats! Clover, it's Riley, it's your boyfr—"

I don't hear the rest, as Riley's scanning the parade as if looking for someone. Then the man turns, and it must be his dad, as his broad, cheeky grin matches Riley's exactly. I no longer care about Riley seeing me in costume. He's dressed up too, after all.

"Riley!" I call out, pulling off my furry headwear. "You didn't tell me you were in the parade!"

"Thought I'd surprise you," he says with a grin.

"Love the wig," I snigger.

"Love the bear suit," he shoots back, adding, "Dad, this is Clover."

"Ah, the musical genius I've heard so much about. Pleased to meet you." He holds out a hand and I shake it with my paw.

"Dad nagged me to do this since he heard about it," Riley explains. "It's not often he gets a chance to dig out the old hippie gear."

"Hey, less of the old," his dad chuckles.

I fall into step with Riley, carried along by the cheers and applause. It no longer matters that I'm being roasted alive in my costume, or that anyone from school could spot me now my face is in full view. Mum and Lily still have their bear heads on, and Mum whoops and waves every time someone cheers our strange little group.

Normally, it feels like years until the parade comes to a halt at the pier. Today, though, it flashes by.

"Did you really do this for your dad?" I ask Riley as the balloon-festooned finish comes into view.

"I didn't have much choice," he says, laughing. "And it's only one day, isn't it?"

"Yeah, guess so." The parade has finished now, and we grab cups of weak orange squash from a table as Mum pulls Lily towards some friends. "Oh, and I heard about your hamburger costume last year," he adds with a grin. *God, did he?* ". . .And I thought, not even Dad's smelly old hippie gear could be as bad as that. . ."

I burst out laughing. "It was pretty bad, believe me."

"Clover!" Lily's voice cuts through the crowd. "Mum says we've got to meet her outside the Ship Inn in five minutes."

My heart crashes. The Ship Inn? I don't want to go to the pub. I want to hang out with Riley and his funny dad. "D'you want to come too?" I ask Riley, with a sudden stab of shyness.

"Sorry, Clover," his dad cuts in, "we're meeting up with the cavemen, then I think everyone's heading down to the beach for a bit of a party. . ." Riley throws me a look which I think means: *sorry.*

"You're welcome to come too," his dad adds quickly, "if it's OK with your mum. Everyone's meeting up at the North Cove. . ."

"Er, I don't think. . ." I start.

"C'mon, Clover," Lily insists, tugging my wrist. "Mum says we've got to go. Maybe we're gonna get our surprise."

And what will it be? A packet of beef-flavoured crisps? A glass of watery lemonade? "I'd better go," I say with a sigh, steering Lily away towards the Ship. Even worse, when I glance back at Riley, Skelling's appeared and jammed herself at his side. She's all teeth and smiles and her short white dress shows off her caramel tan to perfection. Riley's dad's laughing, and now Riley's laughing too, and none of them seems in a terrible hurry to dash off to the cavemen's beach party. Although I could crawl *into* a cave, no trouble at all.

"Come on!" Lily pulls hard on my paw. "Don't you care about Mum's surprise?"

I take a deep breath as we force ourselves through the crowds and into the Ship Inn's beer garden to find Mum. By now, I *do* care about being roasted alive. Don't you see stickers saying "dogs die in hot cars"? Could a person actually die inside a bear outfit – like, drown in their own sweat? That'd give Skelling something to snort about, if I collapsed from overheating in a pile of crumpled fur. Someone might mistake me for a cushion and try to sit on me. They might wonder why it's all knobbly and zip it open and find me, Clover Jones, who might have been a famous musician like her uncle if she hadn't melted on Carnival Day.

Where *is* Mum anyway? Maybe she's gone to the loo. Or she's at the bar ordering iced Cokes for Lily and me.

Then I spot her. Mum, no longer being Daddy Bear but in her normal black jeans and a tight pink top, doing something that makes my stomach lurch.

She's kissing a man. They're standing there, kissing, not like Riley and me, but *slobbery* kissing with their hands all over each other.

"Mum. . ." Lily whispers.

"Shhh!" I hiss.

The leopard dress. Red shoes. Now I get it. This is Mum's little surprise.

Mum's New Friend

"Oh, girls, I didn't see you!" Mum exclaims, blushing furiously as she tears herself away from the lip-sucker.

I gawp at Mum – who looks mortified – then at him. He's short and stocky with shiny pink cheeks like snooker balls. His T-shirt's so tight, you can see all the lumps and bumps of his chest muscles. He looks *corrugated*, like a shed roof. "Um, girls, this is Ed," Mum babbles nervously. "We're, er, friends from the gym and he's been looking forward to meeting you – haven't you, Ed?" She looks around uncomfortably.

Ed nods, sucking in his thin lips. Yeah, he's *really* been dying to meet us.

"This is Clover and Lily," Mum prompts him, to fill the awkward pause.

"Nice to meet you," Ed says gruffly. "Kerry's told me all about you." He picks up a beer from the table and sips it.

Mum takes a desperate swig of her drink. Ed doesn't

say anything else. Obviously, he doesn't want us here. He wants to get on with more vile, slurpy kissing with Mum, who's only been single for what feels like about five minutes.

"I thought today would be a good time for us to get together," Mum gabbles on, snatching her glass and rattling it so the ice cubes chink together. "The carnival's such a special day, isn't it?"

"Yuh," I mumble, my skin prickling in my bear suit. I wonder if Skelling's still primping and posing around Riley, and if she's blagged an invite to the cavemen's beach party yet. Or maybe she and Riley have just snuck off to the other end of the beach together – wasn't that the plan anyway? She's probably got that custard-yellow bikini stashed in her bag, ready to slip on and dazzle him.

Ed clears his throat. "So . . . can I get you girls a drink?"

"Um, Coke, please," I say.

"Me too, please," Lily says nervously.

"Sure," Ed says, disappearing into the pub.

Mum fixes her gaze on me. "You OK, love? You look a bit. . ."

"I'm just hot," I say quickly, struggling out of the bear suit. I still can't believe she got us all excited about a surprise and presented us Ed like a gift.

Mum helps Lily to pull off her costume. Her own outfit's squished into an Iceland carrier bag at her feet.

"How long have you known him?" I ask in a strangled voice.

"Not long, love," Mum says lightly.

"Is he . . . your boyfriend?" Lily demands.

"No, just, er . . . a nice man I've got to know lately. . ." Mum rakes back her hair as Ed struts towards us with our drinks. He hands us our Cokes and glances around the beer garden. "We're all going out for dinner, aren't we, Ed?" Mum says hopefully.

"Oh, are we?" He looks as if he'd rather stab pins in his eyes.

She nudges him. "We said, didn't we, that it'd be a treat after the carnival?"

An idea zings into my brain. Obviously, Mr Muscle doesn't want us around. And if we *are* around – all the time, I mean – he'll realize that Mum, Lily and me come as a package. Then he'll leave Mum alone and everything'll be normal again.

"Would you like that, girls?" Mum asks brightly. "A lovely dinner at the Steak Shack?"

"Yeah," I say. My grin's so fake, it feels like it could fall right off my face.

In the fug of sizzling meat, where the steaks are the size of men's slippers, we learn all about Ed. How he'd spied Mum through the glass partition when she was doing an aerobics class, and hung around by the water cooler until she came out. "He was stalking me," Mum says, laughing.

If it'd been me, I'd have called the police, but she seems to be *flattered*.

"Well," Ed says gruffly, "your mum's a nice lady and we just got chatting." Yeah, right. Having obviously run out of conversation, Ed rips into his lunch like a starved wolf. His steak lolls off either side of his plate and is slathered in onions and gravy. Thank God me and Lily chose nuggets. I wouldn't have managed a tenth of that steak, and then Mum would have started up about food waste and starving children in Africa.

Ed's starting to look more relaxed now, but I know it's an act. You can tell when someone's allergic to young people. They pull a slightly pained face whenever they look at you. Is this how my life's going to be now – with Ed in it, if he's really Mum's new boyfriend? The thought's so horrifying that I need a few minutes to get my head around it.

"Just need the loo," I mutter, grateful to get away from our cosy group. Lily leaps up too, and scuttles across the restaurant behind me, obviously wanting to discuss Ed in minuscule detail. I dive into the ladies' and bolt the cubicle door. I take my time, just sitting there, hoping she'll give up and go back to our table.

"D'you like Ed?" she asks, wide-eyed, as I come out.

"Don't want to talk about it," I mutter as I wash my hands. She tails me out of the loo, and when we turn the corner Mum and Ed are laughing and flirting and touching each other, in a restaurant, where people are *eating*. For some reason she seems to think it's perfectly OK to act like a teenager with this weird little corrugated man.

Seeing us approaching, Mum tries to look all composed and normal again, and Ed fiddles with the bread basket. Those chicken nuggets swirl uneasily in my stomach. Right now, Riley will be at the caveman beach party with Skelling draped all over him.

My meal's gone cold now, and Lily doesn't seem to be terribly interested in hers either. Mum tries her best to keep the conversation flowing, but there are awkward silences that settle over us like dust.

"Anyone fancy dessert?" Ed asks as our greasy plates are finally taken away.

Please say no, Mum, so we can get the hell out of here.

"Shall we share one, Ed?" Mum asks. "And let the girls choose a sundae?"

Although I don't really want dessert, I choose one anyway so I've got something to do other than sit looking at them. Mum and Ed's comes with two long spoons for sharing. Ugh. Thank God they don't start feeding each other. My ice cream slithers down my throat, and I glance around the restaurant at all the normal families, chatting excitedly about the carnival.

And I think about Riley, maybe splashing about in the sea by now, with Skelling in that custard bikini.

"Thank you, Ed," Mum says grandly as he calls over the waitress and pays our bill.

"Thanks," I add as she gives me a quick look, but I don't think he hears me. We all shuffle out, our bear outfits stuffed into carrier bags.

"Well, it was great to meet you, girls," Ed says gruffly outside the restaurant.

I smile bleakly. Lily kicks at a pebble on the ground.

"Thanks, Ed," Mum beams. "That was a fantastic meal. See you soon, OK?"

"Look forward to it," Ed says, before hauling his muscle-bound bulk down the street.

The three of us set off home in silence. "I, um, hope that was OK, girls," Mum says, clearing her throat.

"The food was nice," Lily blurts out.

"Yes, it was," Mum says, taking Lily's hand. "I mean, though, about Ed. . ."

I glance at her as we walk. "You could've warned us," I mumble.

"I know, Clover, but what could I have said? We're just friends, love. But he's a nice guy and I wanted you to meet him instead of keeping it from you. . ."

I shrug. What about that slobbery kissing, then? She doesn't normally do that with her *friends*.

"And to be honest," she continues, "I don't know what'll happen with Ed. It's all very new. It's just . . . nice, you know? Meeting him has cheered me up."

I mull this over, then think about Riley and me: that's pretty new too, and I don't know what's going to happen there either.

"Anyway," Lily adds, gripping her own carrier bag, "next time we go there can I have the sundae with the sparkler in it like that lady had at the next table?"

"Of course you can, sweetheart," Mum laughs, glancing at me. Then her other hand folds around mine, soft and warm, as if trying to convince me that everything's going to be OK.

"Clover, d'you think Mum and Ed'll get married?" Lily whispers in the dark. It's almost eleven p.m. Our light's been off for an hour but I can't sleep. Neither, it seems, can Lily.

I slide my gaze over to her bed. "They've only just met," I hiss back, "and Mum says they're just friends from the gym. . ."

"But they were kissing at the pub!"

"I know, Lil, but maybe . . . it was just all the excitement of the carnival."

I can hear her breath rising and falling as she thinks about this. "I think they love each other, Clover," she adds.

"Well," I say, "maybe they do. Maybe it's all happened really quickly and Ed cheered Mum up after Dad left. But you know what? People don't decide to get married after going out two or three times, so there's nothing to worry about."

There's silence, and I can sense her chewing this over. "If they *do* get married," she pipes up, "d'you think we'll be bridesmaids?"

I snort into my duvet. "Can you honestly imagine Mum ever marrying him?"

"He's got big arms, hasn't he?" she says, giggling.

"Yeah, like tree trunks."

"Or fat barrels," she cuts in, "like the ones outside the Ship Inn that they plant flowers in. . ."

We're both laughing now, and I'm bunching wodges of duvet into my mouth so Mum doesn't hear and come up to tell us to shush. Sometimes, sharing a room with Lily isn't so bad at all.

"Clover. . ." Her voice wavers.

"Uh-huh?"

"Are you sure Ed won't be our new stepdad?"

How do I answer this? Sometimes I think I know less than nothing about adults and the stuff they get up to. "Of course not," I say firmly. "It'll all be over before we know it, and then we'll have our normal mum back again."

Lily wriggles in bed to get comfy, then her breathing steadies and I know she's asleep. It amazes me, how my sister believes me. And for one crazy moment, I almost believe me too.

22

Home Alone

I don't see much of Riley at school on Monday. Everyone's gathered in groups at break and lunchtime, laughing about stuff that happened on Saturday, probably going over every tiny detail of the beach party I couldn't go to because I was being held hostage in the Ship Inn. "So how was the rest of your carnival day?" Riley asks as we head down to Niall's together.

I exhale loudly. "Mum had arranged for us to meet her new man. . ."

"She's met someone already?"

"Sort of looks like it. I don't know if it's serious or anything – I mean, Mum tends to jump into things without thinking, you know? Like the day she walked out of her job. Anyway, we had to sit through this terrible meal and watch him slurping his beer *and* slurping all over Mum. . ." I wince at the image of Ed in his too-tight T-shirt.

Riley smiles sympathetically. "She's probably just

lonely," he suggests. "My dad went out with a couple of women after Mum left, but neither of them seemed keen to hang out with a hairy old hippie like him."

I laugh, even though I can't imagine being so lonely that I'd want anything to do with a pumped-up grunter like Ed. "So what did you do the rest of Carnival Day?" I ask as Niall's house comes into view.

"Oh, just hung out with Dad and some others," he says.

"Like . . . Sophie?" I blurt out.

He turns and gives me a quizzical look. "Yeah, why?"

"I, um, just wondered," I say with an exaggerated shrug.

Riley looks at me, and my cheeks flush hotly. "It was just a beach party, Clover," he says with a laugh. "You should've come."

I can't ask about the beach party after our lesson because Riley's dad picks him up in his car. "I'm popping out for a bit later," Mum explains when I get home, although as she's wearing her sparkly top and short skirt, I'd hardly imagined she was planning a night in front of the telly.

"Are you meeting Ed?" I ask tersely.

She nods, and I feel a twinge of guilt. She looks pretty, with her make-up immaculately applied, and her eyes sparkle with excitement. "I'll only be gone a couple of hours," she adds. "Want me to ask Betty to come over?"

"No, it's all right. I can look after Lily."

Her face breaks into a smile, and she pulls me in for a hug. "You're such a good girl, Clover, you know that?"

I nod wordlessly.

"Sometimes I don't know how I'd manage without you."

I smile awkwardly, not knowing what to say.

In fact, she's out for more than two hours. She went out at eight, and it's nearly midnight when she creeps in, thinking I won't hear her heels clacking on the wooden floor of our hall. From the stillness of my room, I hear a low, rumbly voice too. It's not just Mum – she must have brought Ed back with her. Then music goes on. It's not screamingly loud, but loud enough for me to hear that it's one of Jupe's old records. I don't know why she's picked that one, as Mum stopped playing Jupe's stuff after the terrible thing happened and we all fell out. It was as if she was trying to rub him out of our lives. Maybe Ed likes it, or she's showing off about her famous brother, even though he's dead and she hadn't spoken to him in three years. As far as claims to fame go, it does seem a bit lame.

About an hour later, I hear Ed leaving and Mum padding softly upstairs to bed. Only then can I breathe normally and drift off to sleep.

Dressing-Gown Theft

As Mum still hasn't found a new job, I don't have to collect Lily from school every day any more. "I'm in town anyway," Mum explained, "dropping off job applications to the shops and cafés. So I can start picking her up." Freedom! This means I can head down to the beach if I want, like everyone other normal person my age, before everyone drifts home for dinner.

Today, I'm actually invited round to Jess's. It's not that Jess doesn't want me to come over very often. It's Jess's mum, who's super-strict, and reckons Jess should be huddled over her homework for about six hours a night. I usually have mine done in about ten minutes. "You don't think anything's going on between Riley and Skelling, do you?" she asks, lounging on her pristine cream-coloured duvet amidst a scattering of glossy magazines.

"I don't know," I tell her. "If ever I mention her, he acts like he doesn't want to talk about it. And it's weird –

even when she's being catty and horrible, he's still kind of . . . loyal and nice to her. I mean, I wouldn't want someone like that constantly hanging around me. . ."

"Maybe he's just flattered," Jess remarks.

"Yeah, perhaps that's it. . . Anyway," I say with a shrug, "I'm sick of worrying about Skelling. I've just got too much going now with Mum seeing Ed, and having to go round to Dad's and be all smiley with Bernice. . ."

She nods in sympathy. I glance around Jess's room. Everything's in its place: books neatly lined up on shelves, nail polishes in a tidy arrangement on her dressing table, guitar propped up in the corner of the room (I taught Jess three chords ages ago, but she lost interest after that). As an only child, Jess doesn't have to share.

"You're right," Jess adds. "Who cares about an airhead like that? And Riley obviously likes you. . ."

"Well," I say with a shrug, "I guess he does. He walked through town with me when I was wearing that bear costume. Not a lot of boys would do that."

First thing I see when I get home is a tracksuit top – a *man's* tracksuit top – strewn over our banister. And there's something else. A noise, a terrible growling noise, coming from our bathroom. I stop dead in our hallway and stare up. "*Raaaaaaa!*" it goes, like a wild beast that's broken into our house and is running amok with Mum's wrinkle creams. "*Ma luuurve's extreme!*" the beast roars. "*Outta space, outta ma miiiind. . .*"

Oh God. There's a man up there, in our bathroom – in our shower, judging by the acoustics – belting it out, as if he's Jupe.

"*Ah'd go to Mars for you. . .*" he screams on. "*Jupiter and Saturn too. . .*"

Right now, being teleported to Pluto would suit me just fine. I shut my eyes tightly and try to beam myself there. Lily's draped across the sofa, watching TV, as if this is perfectly normal. Mum appears from the kitchen, oven gloves on her hands, a massive smile on her face. "Have a nice time at Jess's?" she asks.

"Er, yes, thanks. Who's, um . . . up there?"

"Oh, that!" She chuckles as if she's only just registered the terrible warbling. "Ed popped by. He'd been out for a run, then I persuaded him to stay for a while and have some dinner with us. He was a bit sweaty, so I said he could have a quick shower. . ."

"Oh," I choke out. Ed, a bit sweaty. I start to feel a little sick.

"I'm making lasagne," Mum adds cheerfully. "Want some, darling?"

"Er, no, I had dinner at Jess's, thanks." A normal dinner in a normal house. OK, it was slightly tense, with Jess's mum watching us closely to make sure our table manners were up to standard. But still. There was no screaming madman in the shower upstairs.

Mum calls Lily through for dinner, and I park myself in front of the TV. When I peep into the kitchen later, everyone – Lily, Mum, Ed – is assembled happily around the table like some beaming family from a cereal ad. Mum is wearing a new turquoise top and full make-up. Ed is wearing a dressing gown. *Dad's* dressing gown, I realize with a jolt, that he didn't bother taking when he left us. What's Mum thinking, letting him wear it? Because Ed's so much wider than Dad, his vast chest is forcing it open at the front, and a forest of dark, frizzy chest hair sprouts up towards his fat, pink neck.

I scuttle back to the TV. When I look through again, Ed's still at our table, chatting to Mum. "Hi, Clover," he says gruffly, finally noticing me standing there.

"Hello," I snarl. He doesn't even look embarrassed to be here, let alone to be wearing my dad's dressing gown next to his hairy bare-naked skin. As he gets up to fetch the teapot from the worktop, refilling his and Mum's mugs, I realize he looks as if, as if . . . he *lives* here. As if he really is one of us, after knowing Mum for about five minutes. Obviously, Mum having two daughters – one who's trying to zap him with sour vibes from the kitchen doorway – isn't putting him off her one bit. I hear Lily trotting upstairs. A few moments later, the tinny sound of her favourite compilation CD filters down from our room.

"Not long till the summer holidays," Mum says, smiling at me.

"Are we going on holiday?" I ask warily.

Mum grins soppily at Ed, and he winks at her. "Oh, I'm not sure about that. Money's so tight with me not working, love. But I'm sure we'll figure out something." I don't bother quizzing her because if there *is* a plan, and it involves Ed, I'd rather pretend it's not happening so I can mentally spirit myself off to some other place (like Pluto) where Mum is normal again, not a giggling temptress stirring Mr Muscle's tea.

I mean, he pumps iron at the gym, right? And he rips apart entire cows with his teeth. So surely he's capable of handling a tiddly teaspoon all by himself?

24

Play From the Heart

Jess and I head for the beach after school the next day, where Riley and a whole load of boys are messing about with surfboards. There's a pile of school clothes dumped on the beach, and the boys have all changed into surf shorts. "Hope it's OK," I tell Mum on my mobile, trying not to stare as Riley plunges through the waves. "It's just, everyone else was going. . ."

"That's fine, love," she says, sounding all sparkly and happy. "Just be careful and come back by five." In fact, it's such a laugh on the beach – a great gang of us and, even better, no Skelling – that I totally forget the time as we run through the surf and gather up armfuls of driftwood for a fire. When you live at the seaside, you often take it for granted and forget how great it can be. As we all work together to keep the fire going, piling on bits of broken crate, I start to wish the day could stretch on for ever. It's nearly six when I finally get home, and my school trousers are soaking.

"Sorry, Mum," I mumble, expecting a lecture about my precious uniform being ruined.

She sighs, then rolls her eyes good-naturedly. "Well, I suppose it's better you're out in the fresh air than moping about here. You'd better get changed, though, instead of dripping all over the floor."

I'm getting changed in my room when I hear Ed arriving. I get dressed quickly, shovel down my dinner at top speed in front of the TV and hope Mum won't bring him through from the kitchen so we can all sit and have a jolly conversation. My guitar's propped up against the sofa, so I pick it up and start to play.

"How long you been playin', then?" Ed's appeared in the living room clutching a mug of tea.

"Um, since I was about seven," I tell him.

Ed emits a low whistle. "You're not bad. Not bad at all."

"Thanks," I say, sensing a smidgeon of pride.

"Suppose it's in the blood," he adds, "with your uncle and that."

I nod. The last thing I want right now is to be sucked into a conversation about Jupe.

"I love his music, you know," Ed goes on. "Couldn't believe it when I found out he was your mum's brother."

I nod, not knowing what to say.

"Shame they fell out," Ed adds. "You'd think they could've worked it out, don't you?"

"Er, yes," I say in a small voice.

"Guess your mum's pretty stubborn," he adds with a smile.

"Yeah, I suppose she is. But I don't know, really. I've tried to ask why we just lost touch, but she obviously hates talking about it."

Ed nods, taking this in. "Anyway," he adds, brightening, "I like your playing style, Clover. Only. . ." He scratches his round, pink head. ". . .Couldn't you play a bit more. . ."

"A bit more what?"

"Well . . . louder." He grins, and a gold bottom tooth glints. "It'd sound better if you really *went* for it, know what I'm saying?"

I blink at him. "It's an acoustic guitar, Ed. Not electric."

"Uh?" he grunts.

"It's, like, you can't turn it up, unless you've got an electric pickup and amp, which I don't have. You can strum harder, but it's never going to be really loud, if you mean loud like *electric* loud. . ."

"Haven't you got an electric guitar?" Ed asks, frowning.

"Er, no."

"Oh." He looks genuinely crestfallen. "That's a shame. You're a talented girl. Don't they have guitars at school, then?"

"They do," I explain, "but we're not allowed to take them home. And I can't ask Mum for one with her not working at the moment. . ."

"Got a Saturday job?"

I shake my head. "I'm only thirteen. I'm going to help out my guitar teacher with a bit of babysitting, but that's in exchange for my lessons."

Ed nods and sips his tea. "Well, that's pretty resourceful. Can I, um. . ." He hesitates, looking slightly embarrassed. "Could I have a go on that guitar of yours?"

"I . . . I suppose so."

He smiles and sits down beside me on the sofa as I reluctantly hand over my guitar. For once, I'm *so* glad Riley isn't here. "D'you play, then?" I ask.

"A bit. Well, I used to. I'm sure it'll all come back. . ." I frown as Ed starts strumming. Amazingly, he does seem to know a couple of chords, but his great fat sausage fingers keep missing the frets and the strings buzz discordantly. Even so, I sort of recognize the tune he's trying to thrash out. It's an old song, one that's buried deep in my mind and under my skin, that nobody except Jupe and me knew. He never recorded it and, as far as I know, no one else heard it. He called it "Clover's Song".

It's a song I've tried to forget.

I gawp as Ed wallops the strings. "That song," I start, "how d'you know it?" But he can't hear me. Or he doesn't want to. His eyes are scrunched shut, and he's warbling the lyrics now, as if spiriting himself off to some other place – like on stage in front of hysterical fans instead of a scruffy living room.

"Ed!" I try to cut in. "How d'you know that song?"

He grinds to a stop and grins at me. His cheeks are flushed scarlet, and a trickle of sweat runs down his forehead. "Just remembered it from somewhere," he says, catching his breath.

"But . . . it was never recorded or anything. So you *can't* know it. . ." What am I saying? He does know. He even got most of the words right. That's always been my song, and now Ed's stormed into our lives and stolen it.

"Told you I was a big fan," he says with a chuckle.

"Yes, but. . ."

"D'you see what I mean about playing?" he interrupts.

"See . . . what?" I mouth, still all choked up at him playing my song.

"Passion. Energy. That's what you need." He punches his chest. "Music comes from here, Clover. From the heart."

And with that, he gently places the guitar on the sofa and saunters back through to the kitchen to see Mum.

I stare after Ed, the lyrics still ringing in my ears. If it wasn't bad enough having him screeching in our shower and lounging about in Dad's dressing gown, now he's played a song he couldn't *possibly* know and acted all mysterious about it. I glare at my guitar lying across the sofa, and wipe away his sweaty fingerprints with the front of my T-shirt.

"Me and Jupe?" I hear Mum saying. "Oh, don't keep

asking me that, Ed. I already told you. We had . . . an argument, that's all. There was a kind of accident, but it's all so long ago now. . ."

"But what—" Ed starts.

"Please, Ed, darling," Mum cuts in.

I stride into the kitchen, where Ed's helping himself to juice from our fridge. "Heard you playing just then, love," Mum remarks. "Didn't sound like your usual style. . ."

"Oh, that?" Ed chuckles, swigging straight from the carton. "That wasn't Clover. That was me. I was just showing her a thing or two."

Catching my eye, Mum bursts out laughing. "Oh, right. So you're the musical expert, are you, Ed?"

"Not technically, maybe," he says gruffly. "But that's what I was trying to explain to Clover. It doesn't matter about hitting the right notes. Music comes from here, doesn't it?" He raps hard on his chest. "From the heart."

Riley's Secret

I wish someone would explain how things go. Boy kisses you, then you hang out for ages (no more kissing) and *then*, when you've worried like mad that he doesn't want you in his house for some reason, he casually says, "D'you want to bring your guitar over on Saturday?"

So here I am, in Riley's *actual bedroom*. I'd imagined a kind of hippie house with weird fabrics draped everywhere and a smell of incense – but it's just normal. Bit scruffy, few dirty dishes piled up in the sink downstairs, but kind of cosy. Maybe his dad only gets to be a proper hippie on Carnival Day.

"So Ed reckons he's a musical genius?" Riley says, perched on his bed while he tunes up his guitar.

"Looks like it," I say. "Maybe I don't need to go to Niall's after all."

Riley smiles, causing my heart to flap like a bat in my chest.

"Reckon it's serious with them? Your mum and Ed, I mean?"

I shrug. "Well, he obviously likes her. He's always popping in. . ."

"Doesn't he work?" Riley asks.

"He's supposed to. He reckons he's an odd-job man. But he always seems to be just passing our house. . ."

"D'you mind him being around?" Riley asks.

I mull this over. Downstairs, Riley's dad is pottering about in the kitchen. Although there's no mum here, it feels calm and normal compared to our house. "I don't have much choice," I say lightly.

While Riley digs out some music, I glance around his cluttered room. In a corner, propped against the wall, is a cork pinboard crammed with photos. Some look pretty tatty and are curling at the corners. "Are those your old friends?" I ask, indicating beach shots of groups of boys.

"Yeah," he says. "I went through a phase of taking loads of pictures before me and Dad left Haven Bay." I scan the pictures, amazed that a boy would have a pinboard like this (but then, my knowledge of boys' bedrooms is tragically limited).

"Who's that?" I ask, noticing a tiny picture pinned in the bottom corner, of a much younger Riley building sandcastles with a little girl.

"Guess," he says with a grin, placing his guitar on the bed and sitting on the carpet beside me.

"Um, first girlfriend?" I tease.

"Not really. A friend, though. Yeah, definitely my best mate back then. Still don't get it?"

I shake my head. "Haven't a clue. . ."

"Sophie Skelling." He holds my gaze.

"Honestly?" I peer back at the photo, and now he's said it, I can see the younger her. Before custard bikinis. And 34C boobs. She's chubbier, with a fuzz of mousey-brown hair that sticks up at odd angles. In fact, it's even more out of control than mine was, pre-Bernice. "But . . . you mean you knew Sophie when you were little?"

Riley nods. "Yeah."

"Why didn't you ever say?" I blurt out. I can't believe it. It's as if all of a sudden, he's not the boy I thought he was. Couldn't he have mentioned that he knew her back then? I didn't even know Skelling came from Haven. No wonder she looks at me like she'd happily stab me with her mascara wand!

"It's kind of complicated," he says, shifting position on the carpet.

"But, Riley, I've told you *everything* about me – all the Jupe stuff, Mum and Ed . . . everything." I shake my head, trying to make sense of it all. "No wonder Sophie's so weird and hostile with me," I add, seized by an urge to storm out of Riley's room and go home.

"She's not what you think," Riley says quietly.

"How d'you know what I think?" I snap, leaping up

and grabbing my guitar. "I think she's got a big problem with me. That's all I know, and you're obviously trying to play a game with me. Do you and Sophie laugh about me behind my back?"

"Of course we don't!" Riley protests, jumping up too. "Our parents were close friends, OK? But there's other stuff I can't tell you. I just can't. I'm sorry, Clover. . ."

I can still see that photo out of the corner of my eye. It's as if she's laughing at me, without even being here. "Well," I snap, "I'm sorry too. And I'm going home."

We're standing so close, I can feel his warm breath on my face. I leave a small space where he's meant to explain everything, like why he hasn't been honest with me. But he doesn't. "All right," he murmurs.

"See you, then," I say, my lip wobbling. Riley nods and I leave his room and hurry downstairs and out into the street, without saying goodbye to his dad.

Whatever's going on between Riley and Skelling, it's obviously far more important than me. Well, I don't need friends like him – friends who keep whopping secrets and string you along and end up making you feel bad. "Have a nice life," I mutter, blinking away furious tears as I march home.

26

The Letter

At home, Mum and Ed are snuggled up together like lovebirds on the sofa. Lily's at a birthday party, so God knows how much snogging and mauling's been going on while I've been out. Ed's arm is slung around Mum's shoulders, and she's resting her head against his chest. I imagine it'd be as comfy as having a paving slab for a pillow.

"Everything OK?" Mum asks, having the decency to disentangle herself.

"Yep," I say curtly, turning to head up to my room.

"Um, stay down here for a minute, would you?" she adds. "I . . . I've got something to tell you."

"What is it?" I ask hesitantly.

Mum glances at Ed, as if needing reassurance. "It's about Jupe, love. . ."

I swallow hard. "What about him?"

"Um, it's come as a bit of a shock. I've had a letter from a solicitor. He's been dealing with Jupe's will and it's taken him a bit of time to track us down."

I frown, trying to make sense of this. Has he left us something? I can still picture Crickle Cottage with its shabby sofas and worn-out rugs. I can't imagine what he'd want us to have.

"Clover," Mum continues, her eyes misting now, "you know me and Jupe were really close, don't you, until . . . the thing happened?"

"Yes. . ." My heart flips over. I think about that letter I wrote after Mum told me he'd died, which is tucked under my socks in my drawer. No one ever remembers that I lost him too.

A lone tear drips down Mum's cheek. "It's all right," Ed says gently. "Don't get upset, Kerry. . ."

Swiping her sleeve across her face, Mum picks up a letter from the coffee table and hands it to me.

I read:

For the Attention of Mrs Kerry Jones

This is to inform you that I have been appointed as executor for the estate of the late Mr Jupiter Hughes. Mr Hughes has named you as the beneficiary in his will and testament to the effect that he wished you to have the entire contents of his rented home, Crickle Cottage, at Herring Point, Hicklow, North Cornwall. A condition attached to the will is that you take responsibility for the clearing of the house. The owner is anxious that the house is cleared within two months, so I would be obliged if you could contact me as soon as possible.

Yours faithfully,
Mr Eric Barlow, solicitor acting on behalf of the late Mr Jupiter Hughes

I know this is something big. So big, in fact, that I don't know what to do apart from blurt out, "What does beneficiary mean?"

"Clover," Mum says gently, "it means that, for some reason, and I haven't the faintest idea why, Jupe's left everything to us."

For a moment, I panic that we'll have to leave Copper Beach and move into Crickle Cottage. It's a free house, isn't it? Jupe left it to us. And I know how short of money we are these days. "I'll have to change schools!" I exclaim. "I won't know anyone and—"

"Clover," Mum cuts in, placing a hand on my arm, "don't worry, sweetheart. We're not moving anywhere. And Jupe's will – it's probably no big deal. The other band members invested their money and got into management and stuff. But Jupe – well, I don't think he had much by the end. It's probably just a few bits and bobs."

"But what about the cottage?" I ask, my head swimming. I'm so glad Lily's not here. It's hard enough to get a grip on what's happening without her firing questions.

"Jupe didn't own Crickle Cottage," Mum explains gently. "It was rented, love. Look, it says here in the letter."

"Oh," comes my mouse-sized voice.

"It does mean we'll have to go on a trip to Jupe's, though," Mum adds.

"Why?" I ask.

"To sort through his things," Ed explains, "and see if there's anything we want."

"*We?*" I exclaim. "Are you coming too?" Mum throws Ed a sharp glance and he looks sheepishly at the floor.

"I just mean I'd be happy to help sort everything out," he mutters.

"Well, we could all go, I suppose," Mum adds, her voice wobbling slightly. "We could go for a week, make a sort of holiday out of it. . ."

My stomach twists uneasily. I want to go back, to see Jupe's cottage again after all these years. Yet it feels a bit creepy, having a holiday in my dead uncle's house. A shiver runs through me.

Mum frowns, beckoning me on to the sofa beside her. "Are you OK, Clover? I know this is upsetting for you. . ."

I nod. "I'm fine, Mum. It's just all a bit weird. . ."

"Yes, I know."

"What about Fuzz?" I ask suddenly.

"Fuzz?" Mum looks confused.

"Jupe's cat, remember?"

"Yes, of course." She musters a smile. "Well, it's three years since we saw Jupe and Fuzz was getting on by then, so maybe he died a while ago. . ."

"But what if he's not dead?" I blurt out. "What if he's roaming about with no one to look after him?"

Mum pulls me close. Thankfully, Ed has edged away to the far end of the sofa. "You know what cats are like," she says. "They're always going off and finding other families to look after them. I'm sure, if Fuzz is still alive, he's found himself a nice new home."

I look at Mum and Ed, and try to imagine us all cooped up in Jupe's house for a whole week. "It'll be an adventure, won't it, Kerry?" Ed adds, turning to Mum.

"Will it?" I ask.

"Well . . . yeah! Seeing all his stuff, his guitars and all that . . . it'll be amazing!"

"I've seen all Jupe's stuff loads of times," I say coolly.

"Don't be like that, Clover," Mum says, frowning.

"Sorry," I mumble, realizing now what Ed has in mind for our trip. He's planning to get his hands on my uncle's guitars. And the thought of him wailing and *playing from the heart* in Crickle Cottage almost makes me wish Jupe had left us nothing at all.

Hamster Horror

We're leaving school on Monday lunch time when Skelling catches up with Jess and me. She's wearing thick lipgloss that has a sparkly (and, I have to say, *cheapening*) effect, and so much mascara she could trigger a hurricane just by blinking.

"Hey, Clover," she sneers. "Going anywhere nice for your holidays?"

Jess throws me a *just-rise-above-it* look.

I try to mentally raise myself, but remain firmly planted on the hot school tarmac.

"You deaf or something?" Skelling snarls. "Been playing your guitar so much you've damaged your eardrums?"

"We haven't made any plans yet," I say airily.

"We break up on Friday, you know," she adds. She's working up to something here, and I don't like it one bit.

"Yeah," I say, "I do know that."

Small pause for effect. "We're going to France. My parents have a holiday house there."

"Big deal," Jess mutters. Everyone knows about her French house because when her parents bought it, she talked about nothing else. She even brought in the estate agent's details and flashed them around as if they'd bought Buckingham Palace.

Skelling chomps her gum noisily. "C'mon, Clover," Jess says, nudging me.

I turn and fall into step with her, conscious of Skelling glaring at the backs of our heads. "Anyway," she calls after us, "it's gonna be great this year 'cause we're going for the whole summer holidays."

"Poor France," I snort.

"Yeah," Skelling crows across the yard, "it'll be the best ever. Didn't Riley tell you he's coming too?"

"She's lying," Jess hisses as we speed-walk to the canteen. "He would have told you, wouldn't he?"

"Probably not," I say airily, "seeing as he hadn't even told me that he and Skelling used to play on the beach and build sandcastles together back in Haven. . ."

"I can't believe he'd even want to go," Jess reasons, snatching a greasy tray. "He's getting sick of the way she's always leeching around him. You can tell."

I exhale loudly and plonk a plain cheese baguette on to my tray. I don't have the stomach for anything more "experimental", not after that cheese soufflé topping that slopped around in my stomach for about a week.

"Or maybe," Jess continues, "it was too good an offer to turn down. Free holiday and all that. Bet his dad can't afford to take him abroad. . ."

"But it still means he's going to be stuck with—" I stop myself as Skelling marches into the canteen with Riley at her side. Steering Jess to a table in the furthest corner of the canteen, I try to convince myself that the pair of them *aren't* discussing the fabulous time they're going to have in France.

By the time I get home, I've managed to get a grip on myself. I've made a mental list of all the positive things about Riley going to Skelling's French palace and they are as follows:

1. Have spent far too much time angsting over Riley and the thought of not having him around is almost a relief. I said . . . *almost*.
2. I don't want 34C boobs like Skelling's. Why would I? It's fantastic being so flat that, when a man bumped into me in Tony's chippie, he looked at me in my beanie and said, "Sorry, sonny."

I realize now that point two is not a positive reason or, in fact, anything to do with France at all. But who cares? I'll have a fantastic holiday sorting through Jupe's possessions with music tuition from Ed thrown in. Can't wait.

So I'm feeling pretty bold as I march round to Riley's after dinner and rap firmly on his front door. No one answers. I peep in through the living room window and scan the dining table laden with newspapers and coffee cups.

I knock again. My heart hop-skips with the stress of being kept waiting. I'm about to leave when there's a shuffling noise inside. The door opens, and there's Riley, ruffle-haired with beautiful, toffee-coloured skin. His eyes, though, aren't beautiful any more. They are hard.

"Um, hi," I say, taken aback by his coldness. "I left my guitar strap in your room and wondered if you'd found it."

"Right," he says flatly. "I'll just go and look." He disappears, leaving me standing on the doorstep, and reappears with my strap.

"Thanks," I mumble. There's an awkward pause, and I have to keep my mouth tightly shut to stop myself from asking him about France.

"Um, is that it?" he asks.

"Guess so." I take a deep breath. It doesn't feel right, us being like this. I wish I'd never seen that photo, never gone on about Skelling, never acted like such an idiot by marching out of his house. She's ruined everything – just as she wanted to. Why couldn't I have just played guitar with him and never mentioned her at all?

"Riley?" calls his dad from upstairs. "Who is it?"

Riley doesn't answer. He just keeps shooting me a cool look. In fact, it's an *icy* look that chills my bones. "I, um . . . shouldn't have stormed off the other day," I say quietly. "I was just a bit . . . surprised, that's all."

"It doesn't matter," he snaps. "Anyway, I'm a bit busy right now." He steps back into the hallway as if preparing to slam the door in my face.

"Fine, then. See you around, if you're so *busy*. . ." I inhale deeply, determined to show no emotion. I fail pathetically because my left eye's vibrating madly, and tears are threatening to well up.

"Who's at the door?" his dad calls out again as I turn and walk away from the house.

"Nobody," Riley yells back.

Nobody?

The word rings in my ears. Nobody. *You're nobody, Clover Jones.*

I don't look back because I'm too busy running. I run down Riley's road and along the seafront and up the steep hill to our street. I burst in through our front door, into our hall and then our living room where I skid on something brown and furry, which sends my foot flying up and me tumbling backwards against the TV. "Clover!" Lily screams. "You stupid idiot! You've trodden on Cedric! You've *killed* him!"

I collapse forward with my hands over my face.

Clever, brilliant Cedric who I've had since I was eleven. Oh my God.

I daren't look. My poor, defenceless animal who was perfectly happy scampering through his tunnels and on his exercise wheel. I *murdered* him.

At least it was a quick death. And painless, I hope. Tears spring from my eyes and stick to my hot, damp fingers. I feel like I'm completely liquefying.

"What's happened?" Mum cries, charging into the living room.

"Cedric!" I wail over Lily's sobs. "I've killed Cedric!" Fat tears are dribbling down my cheeks.

"Um, Clover. . ." Mum ventures, her mouth twitching as Ed saunters in.

"I'm sorry!" I croak. "I'm really, really sorry. I just ran in and didn't see him. . ."

"Clover, sweetheart. Listen to me." Mum puts an arm around me. "It's OK. You didn't kill him. . . That wasn't Cedric."

Slowly, I remove my hands from my face and dare to scan the floor. I'm expecting blood and crushed bones. Maybe a tiny heart, still beating. "So what . . . what was it?" I whisper.

Mum's smiling now. "It's one of the ears from Lily's bear costume. It fell off and she put it there to play a joke on you."

I glare at Lily, who's quit her fake hysterics and is giggling madly. "Very funny," I snap. "Very, very funny!"

"Sorry," she splutters.

"Oh, Clover, it was just a joke," Mum says.

Just a joke? Do they think this is what I need right now? I barge upstairs, where I grab my guitar and fix on my strap and start strumming and strumming, trying to shut everything out – custard bikinis and Riley Hart and our almost-squished hamster. I play and play, as loud as I can, thrashing the strings as a new song pours out. I stop, breathless, my heart juddering.

"Hey, Clover!" Ed calls upstairs. "See you've taken on board what I told you, yeah? *Now* you're playing from the heart."

Back to Crickle Cottage

A week later, the summer holiday's started and Riley hasn't spoken to me since I collected my guitar strap. Not that I care. Let him hang about with Skelling if she means that much to him. Real friends don't keep secrets about their past, and they don't have French holidays planned and not tell you. I'm sick of trying to guess everything, and anyway, something much more important than Riley is about to happen. I'm going back to Jupe's place for the first time in three years.

We're heading there now, in Ed's rusty white van. The writing on the side of his van says NO JOB TOO BIG OR TOO SMALL and there's a picture of a man with a hammer. I reckon most jobs *are* either too big or too small, because Ed never seems to have one.

The whole journey so far, he's blabbed on about Jupe. Like, what was the big fallout about, anyway? (Mum makes vague noises that maybe a bird could interpret, but they're not on any human frequency.)

"I mean, imagine having a talent like that in the family. . ." Ed emits a low whistle. Mum stares out at the pastel blue sky.

The four of us are lined up on the van's cracked leather front seat – illegally, as there aren't enough seatbelts – and Lily keeps jabbing her elbow into me. "Stop it," I mutter.

"I'm not doing anything!" she protests.

"Cheer up, Clover," Mum barks. "We're going on *holiday*."

I try to, I really do. I focus on all the good things I remember about Jupe's place, like Silver Cove with its soft white sand, and the rock pools where we found a starfish.

We've been driving for over two hours when we stop outside the solicitor's office in a small, dreary-looking town. As Mum goes in to pick up the key, I close my eyes and try to taste the vanilla ice cream that Jupe would buy us when we walked up to the village. But ice cream sets me thinking about Skelling and Riley in France, and now I'm imagining them licking from the same cone and that makes me feel really sick.

"Come on, love, crack a smile," Mum insists, climbing back into the van. "You look like you're going to a funeral."

Which we are, in a way, as we didn't go to Jupe's real funeral. We only found out he'd died after it was over.

The couple who ran the ice cream shop in the village had remembered us coming on visits, and together with Jupe's landlord, they'd found our phone number and called Mum. So it's only when we're out in open countryside again, and I spot Crickle Cottage perched on the hill, that it hits me that he's really dead. It seems impossible that we're coming to stay at his house and he won't be there.

My skin tingles as we approach it and pull up on the small oval of gravel. We clamber out of the van. Crickle Cottage is stranded all on its own, as if no other houses wanted to play with it. There's no garden or wall – just a bit of rickety fence that's half fallen down.

"So this is it," Ed marvels, gazing around.

Mum nods and smiles, but even she looks nervous as she pulls out the key. "OK, love?" she asks brightly.

"Yes," I squeak.

Then she opens the front door, and it all comes whooshing back in my face.

All the memories.

Me, Mum, Dad, Lily and Jupe, all together, listening while Jupe plays a song. The late nights, when Lily was tucked up in bed, but I was allowed to stay up like one of the grown-ups. Jupe's cat hissing at me, and me being obsessed with trying to befriend it.

Taking a deep breath, and conscious of Lily slipping her hand into mine, I step into the past.

★

It even *smells* dead, although Jupe died in hospital and not, thankfully, in this house. Following Mum into the hallway, I blink in the gloom.

There's a dingy kitchen, living room and bedroom downstairs, all dulled by dust and shadows. The cottage seems smaller than I remembered, maybe because I'm bigger now.

"It's spooky," Lily whispers as we follow Mum from room to room. She's right. You almost expect horrible sinister laughter to burst out of a cupboard. It didn't used to feel creepy. It was filled with music and fun, as if there was always a family party going on. Jupe would hand round his mysterious dark red punch for the adults – Dad called it rocket fuel – and cakes from the village bakery for Lily and me.

"So what d'you think?" Mum asks Ed.

"It's fantastic," he marvels. I notice he keeps touching ordinary things like door handles and light switches, as if some of Jupe's skin cells might transfer on to him, and then he could sell them on eBay.

We all troop upstairs. On the staircase wall is a framed gold disc: "Presented to Falcon" – Jupe's band – "to commemorate the sale of more than one million copies of the album *Shooting Star*". A million copies!

"Amazing," Ed says, and I open my mouth to protest as he reaches out to lift it from the wall.

"Oh, Ed, please leave that just now," Mum says quickly. "Come on, let's check out the other bedrooms."

I throw him a filthy look. He's probably planning to sell that on eBay as well. What else is he going to want to get his paws on?

"Lily, why don't you have this room?" Mum suggests in one of the bedrooms. "And Clover, you have the one you both used to share. That way you'll have your own space."

"OK," I say, shivering. A room of my own, for the first time since Lily was born! I should be over the moon.

We spend the rest of the afternoon down on the beach, and it starts to feel good, being here. Collecting driftwood and helping to build a fire takes my mind off Skelling and Riley for a while. I don't even mind when Mum and Ed go paddling hand-in-hand in the sea.

"Having a nice time?" Dad texts me.

"Yes, great," I reply, which is almost true, especially when Ed drives off to the village to buy fish and chips for all of us. Later, though, as the shadows fall, the cottage starts to feel eerie again. We try to watch TV, but something's wrong with the aerial and the picture's too blurry.

"Well," Mum says with a big, brave smile, "I reckon we might as well all go to bed."

Lily and I head upstairs, and she looks all excited, tucked up in the tiny, lumpy bed. But I can't sleep. The house groans and creaks, and the wind whips through the trees down at the shore. In fact, I wish I was back with Lily in our own bedroom at home, or at least sharing here, like we used to. The sheets smell old and kind of biscuity. My mind swirls with worries, like will Betty remember to feed Cedric? Of course she will. She's a pet person. Wasn't Midnight the most pampered cat in Copper Beach?

There's a squeak on the landing. My heart jolts. I open one eye as a dark shape looms in the doorway. "H-hello?" comes my trembly voice.

There's a dull thumping in my ears and I'm almost expecting to see him standing before me. Jupe, asking, "Who's that idiot man in my house? What does he want with my things?"

"Who is it?" I whisper.

"Clover! Are you awake?"

Sweat springs from my brow, trickling sideways towards the ancient pillow.

"It's me," Lily hisses.

"God, Lily!" I almost pass out with relief.

"I . . . I'm scared, Clover. . ."

"What are you doing, creeping about?"

"I couldn't sleep!" she protests.

"Don't be silly," I say sternly. "There's nothing to be scared of."

"It *feels* scary. Every time I start falling asleep I get worried that I'm gonna have a bad dream. Is . . . is Jupe's house haunted, d'you think?"

"No," I say firmly. "Definitely not. It feels totally *fine*, OK? Just go to sleep."

She steps towards me, looking small and skinny in her candy-striped nightie. "Clover . . . can I sleep in your bed?"

I open my mouth to say no, and that we're far too old to be sharing a titchy single bed. Then there's a horrible creak, and she lurches towards me with something cobwebby stuck to her hair and dives under my covers. "Move over!" she demands.

"You'd better not kick and wriggle," I warn her.

"Promise." She snuggles close to me, still smelling vinegary from the fish and chips. "Clover," she adds, "you're so brave. I'm glad I've got a sister like you."

"Just go to sleep," I say. I don't confess that I'm sleeping in my socks, knickers and T-shirt in case I have to make an emergency getaway in the night.

29

Fishy Business

By the time I come downstairs in the morning, Lily's already prancing about the kitchen in her swimming costume, while Mum and Ed are poring over ancient photos and newspapers at the kitchen table. "Can we go swimming now?" Lily demands.

"After breakfast," I tell her, picking up a faded photo of Jupe's band. There were four members of Falcon – gangly men in regulation tight leather trousers with long hair straggling over their shoulders. The band is crammed into a tiny room with a sloping roof. There's an ashtray balanced on a crate, and there are so many smoking ciggie butts in it, it looks like a mini volcano.

It's weird seeing Jupe like this – so much younger, not nearly as worn-out looking, his eyes almost smouldering against his pale skin.

"The man himself," Ed murmurs. Mum's mouth is set in a tight line as she gathers up the photos.

"I want to go swimming," Lily moans, pacing the room. "When can we go? You *promised*."

"Later, OK?" I pick up a copy of the *Tipden Times*, which must be the local paper around here, and flip through it. Jupe's on page two. It's not the young, pale-faced Jupe, but the old, ravaged Jupe – the one whose entire face crinkled when he laughed, the Jupe *I* knew. My stomach twists uncomfortably.

"You said we'd go swimming," Lily mutters.

I shut off my ears and focus hard on the picture. Jupe's wearing a weird pointy hat. There's an interview with him, which goes like this:

Can you remember the first time you picked up a guitar?

I was seven years old.

What was the turning point for you, musically?

Meeting Robert, Mitch and Chris and forming Falcon.

(As you can gather, Jupe wasn't exactly big on chat with reporters.)

What were your influences?

Various stuff.

What inspired you?

Touring.

How did you feel when Falcon split up?
Bad.

I almost laugh at how little he gave away. They were famous, for God's sake. Girls threw underwear at them. There's that gold disc on the wall. Didn't Jupe have *anything* to say? The other guys ended up with houses all over the world – one even owns an island, according to Mum – and what did Jupe have? This tiddly cottage (which wasn't even his) and a mean cat (whereabouts unknown).

If I ever manage to find people to play with, and form a real band, I'll babble on so much in interviews that the poor journalist will eventually stuff a sock in my mouth and witter, "Thank you, Clover, that's really enough. You've been very honest and enlightening. Now if I can just ask Riley some questions. . ."

Before Riley decided I was worse than a bit of dirt on his shoe, I'd even started to wonder if we could be in a band together one day. He'd need tons of practice but I'd looked forward to spending loads of time helping him.

So, Riley, the reporter would say, **what first brought you and Clover together?**
Riley: It started at school, really. We became friends and would get together to practice, though I was pretty hopeless until Clover helped me get it together.

Does your personal relationship ever cause problems with the band?

Me, yanking sock from mouth: No, never. In fact, it's probably helped, us being so in tune with each other because we write most of our songs together. . .

Riley: It's a good thing, definitely. [Blushes cutely.]

So would you say you're soulmates?

Me: Oh yes!

Riley: Yeah, definitely. [Throws adoring look.]

Thank you, Clover and Riley, for your time today. I wish you much success with your new album.

"Clover!" Lily roars in my ear. "Stop reading and come swimming."

"Oh, let's go too, Ed," Mum announces. "The cove's so pretty and I'm sick of looking through all this old paperwork. It's depressing."

I wish they wouldn't. The thought of Ed in the tight, shiny trunks I've seen draped over our radiator curdles my blood. But there's no escape. We all head down the steep, winding footpath to Silver Cove. Mum and Ed have even brought Jupe's old fishing rods which they found under his bed. They're sleeping in the downstairs bedroom, which used to be his room. Wouldn't that creep you out, sleeping in a dead man's bed? Yet it doesn't seem to bother Mum one bit. I guess she has brave Mr Muscle to protect her from ghouls and stuff.

Ed's first to strip down to his swimmies, plunging in with a massive splash. Mum follows, shrieking with laughter as the water engulfs her. I charge in after Lily, the sea's sudden coldness snatching my breath. By my third stroke, though, the cool water feels soothing. I swim away from the others, playing that newspaper interview over in my head.

If Jupe's life changed when he found his band members, how can I find mine? What chance is there of unearthing a soulmate at Horsedung – especially now that Riley's decided he wants nothing to do with me? *Wait until you're unleashed on the world*, Jupe said once. Maybe I don't need Riley. Surely I can find other people to play with – people who don't mess me around. I *have* to do it, I tell myself as I swim back to shore. I promised Jupe, to make up for the thing I did. It's one promise I intend to keep.

By the time Lily and I emerge from the sea, Mum and Ed are trying to catch our lunch with Jupe's fishing rods. It's not going well. First the float hits a rock and smashes, then the line tangles up in a bush. "Bloody hell," Ed barks, and Mum throws back her head and laughs. At least she's happy. I haven't seen her laugh like this for so long, even before Dad left.

There's nothing to eat at lunchtime apart from bread rolls (which they'd brought for us to have with the fish. Honestly, Ed was that confident about catching one).

"Great fish, Ed," I mutter, my mouth stuffed with dry bread.

He looks at me, and his eyes crinkle. "Yeah, pretty good, isn't it?"

"Really fresh," Mum enthuses, perched on a rock.

"D'you have any more?" Lily giggles.

"Here," he says, passing around his invisible catch. Our eyes meet, and he grins. I still can't believe Mum's replaced Dad so quickly, and I'd slightly prefer it to be just me, Mum and Lily on this beach. But things could be worse. At least we're here, in the sunshine, doing what Jupe asked us to do. And it's *almost* taking my mind off Riley and Skelling in France.

Next day, Ed seems to have accepted that catching a live fish might be a teeny bit trickier than buying one in Asda. We're armed with sausages and firelighters for a barbie, plus a heap of old newspapers from the cottage (I checked each one carefully for any more interviews with Jupe. I don't like the thought of burning him).

"Hey, Clover," Ed says, chomping a sausage, "haven't heard you playing your guitar much here. You did bring it, didn't you?"

"Yeah," I say. "Just haven't felt like it." I don't tell him that I want to play my own, rather than having him butting in like my unofficial teacher.

Ed frowns. "You know, I thought we might have

found Jupe's guitars lying about the house. Me and you could've had a jam."

Jamming with Ed? I'd rather jam my head in a wardrobe door. "Maybe he sold them," I suggest, "or gave them away when he started to get ill. What d'you think, Mum?"

"What? Oh, I don't know," she says vaguely, poking our fire with a piece of driftwood. I don't get her at all. All those times we came here – all those holidays – when there'd be music blasting and impromptu parties. Mum didn't even mind that Fuzz, Jupe's cat, made her eyes itch and her nose run, and that sometimes she'd have to go outside for great gulps of salty air.

We all loved it, until that last, horrible time. Then we never saw him again. How can you just cut someone off like that? I knew Mum was angry with Jupe, but surely you don't fall out with your own brother for ever over one incident? She doesn't even seem to be sorting through his stuff like she's meant to. Isn't this why we're here? To make everything right, like a proper ending in a book?

Maybe she wants to forget what happened. The trouble is, I just can't.

The Worst Day

I'm ten years old and Mum and Dad are still together and everything's normal. There are no shiny swimming trunks on our radiator, and no Nudie Bernice.

And it's Christmas. Not actual Christmas day, as we always spent that at home, but a few days before it. Jupe has a mad-looking tree that he dug up illegally from someone's field, and it's laden with decorations made by me and Lily from cardboard and glitter.

It's just after lunch and Dad and Jupe are already a little bit drunk. Jupe's made his rocket-fuel red punch for the grown-ups, and he's ladling it into glasses from a huge silver pot like a cauldron. Although Mum usually has some, she's recovering from a stomach bug and sipping mugs of tea.

"Hey, Clover, wanna see my new guitar?" Jupe asks.

"Yes, please," I say, delighted. He's let me play all his guitars. They're all battered and scratched and each one feels a little bit different. I can already play about twenty songs.

He fetches a case and opens it. Everyone gathers round and *ooh*s and *ahh*s, although I don't think anyone can figure out why he's so excited about this one. It's electric, burnished orange fading to gold in the middle, like a sunset. Jupe tells me to sit down, plugs the guitar into the amp and hands it to me.

"Was it hundreds of pounds?" I ask nervously.

Jupe chuckles. "No, sweetheart. It was a Christmas present."

"Who from?"

He mentions a name I've never heard of, but even as a kid I can tell it's his hero. Maybe even the person who started *him* playing. I don't know. Anyway, his eyes gleam like emeralds (he has green eyes like me). "Why did he give it to you?" I ask.

"He's been ill for a while and can't play any more," he says. "He thought I'd look after it and appreciate it. Anyway, have a try. I think you'll notice a difference."

I shrink away as he hands it to me.

"Are you sure about this, Jupe?" Mum cuts in. "If it's that special, I'd hate anything to happen. . ."

"Oh, I trust Clover," he declares, and he's

definitely a bit drunk by now. His lips are stained scarlet from the punch, like hair-hacker Babs' mouth while she's been downing red wine with Mum. It looks funnier on Jupe, like badly applied lipstick. "Here you go," he adds. "You're a natural, you are."

I take the guitar and Jupe positions my fingers to form a chord. I start to strum – tentatively at first, as if it might bite me, then more confidently as Jupe eggs me on. "C'mon, Clover," he says, "don't be scared of it."

Soon I'm playing and playing, and Mum and Dad even get up and dance, even though Mum's still not well and Dad *never* dances. Jupe and Dad are slurping red punch, and Jupe gets up to dance too, and Fuzz scurries out through the cat flap because loud music freaks him out and he really should have an owner who plays something soft and gentle, like a harp. Everyone's laughing, and Mum gives me this huge grin, as if she's so proud that I can do this.

And I *am* proud. I look round and see Lily, who only started school a few months ago, whirling around in a princess dressing-up outfit. She's wearing a paper crown and Mum's sparkly clip-on earrings and is clutching a plastic cup with one of those crazy straws sticking out of it. The ones where you can see your drink scooting round the wiggly bits.

Gradually, she makes her way to the table where the punch cauldron is. At first I don't realize what she's up to. I just think she's doing a funny dance. Jupe is too – he's pretty drunk by now, turning up the volume and slugging another cup of punch. Nobody except me notices as Lily dunks her cup into the punch, brings it up to her mouth and takes a huge suck on her crazy straw.

Red liquid shoots up. "Lily, no!" I scream, leaping up from my seat as Jupe's guitar falls from my hands and hits the stone floor. The neck splits, and the whole body cracks, a shattered sunset at my feet.

I stare down at it, frozen in horror.

"What have you done?" Jupe slurs, nearly sending me flying as he pushes me aside in his hurry to get to the guitar.

"Jupe, I—" I cry out, but no other words come.

"Stupid girl!" he roars, like I've never heard him before. I've never seen him this drunk before either. He's scary, and I back away to the furthest corner of the room. Now he's scrabbling on the floor, snatching the broken pieces and *still* yelling at me, Mum, all of us. Mum's screaming back that it wasn't my fault, I'm only a child, and how dare he speak to me like that? And she goes for him – really tries to hit him – but Dad grabs her and tries to calm her down. She's writhing madly like a wild cat, trying to break free. Lily's dropped her cup and is wailing loudly. I stand and stare and wish I could die.

Somehow, in the scuffle, the cauldron's knocked over and the floor's swimming with red liquid. It looks like blood. Then Mum's shouting, "Come on, everyone!", and we're all bundling out of Crickle Cottage and Lily throws up red punch sick all over the scrubby ground. We pile into our bashed-up old car and drive away with Mum raging, "For God's sake, it was only a guitar."

"I still feel sick," Lily whimpers. "Will I die?"

"Of course not, my love," Mum says firmly, turning to Dad. "It's ridiculous, Geoffrey, him having booze about the place with Lily around. . ."

Dad gives her a look, and I can tell what he's thinking: *But it's always like that at Jupe's.* I put my arms around Lily and pull her close to my chest.

Mum blames Jupe for what happened next, even though he isn't even here with us. She blames him for the fact that she takes a corner too fast, veering off the road and through a wooden fence that cracks over our windscreen, flying past us in bits. I can't remember if Lily and I are crying, or what we're doing, because it's all blurry as she screams and swerves. The car seems to bounce over bumps and finally stops in the field. For a moment, there's silence. Then Mum turns, saying, "God, are you all right, girls? Clover, Lily?" over and over again.

"Everyone's fine," Dad tries to reassure her, and we stagger out and stand there, all four of us hugging one another in the middle of a soggy field. When Mum finally peels herself off us and tries to start the car, the wheels spin and spin, stuck in mud. She revs so hard, the car makes a weird kind of spluttering noise, as if it's actually drowning. Then it stops, and no matter how many times she tries, Mum can't get our old car to start again. She won't call Jupe either, even though we're stranded. "I never want to speak to him again," she snaps.

In the end, it's a farmer who comes to help us – the farmer whose fence Mum drove right through. He takes us back to his farm, and calls a local garage so they can tow our car out of the field and check it out. While we wait in the farm kitchen, a man from the garage calls Mum to say some vital engine part's burnt out. Our car is officially dead. "How will we get home?" Lily keeps crying.

"I'll take you to the train station," the farmer says. On the way, we stop off at the garage to collect all our stuff from the car – our suitcases, Lily's cuddly rabbit and even our buckets and spades.

"Nice holiday?" an old lady asks Lily across the aisle on our train journey home.

"Our car crashed," she blurts out.

"Oh, did it?" The lady looks horrified. "Are you all OK?"

"We're fine, thanks," Mum says quickly, squeezing my hand and turning to look out at the stormy grey sky.

We spend the rest of the journey in dazed silence.

And that's the last we ever see of Jupe.

Surprise Visitor

Dear Jupe,
I don't know why I'm sitting up in the middle of the night writing this letter in bed. Maybe it's because I so want to talk to you and this feels like the next best thing. It feels weird staying in Crickle Cottage without you. But I realize we had to come. You made us when you wrote your will. You wanted us to clear out your house (did we ever realize what a mammoth task that was going to be?). We're sorting and taking box after box to the charity shop in Polcreek. Ed keeps saying it's mad, and that your stuff'd be worth a fortune – even your ordinary things like an old ciggie lighter or a pair of wellies with a hole in. He says we should eBay it. Mum won't listen. She says she wants things sorted as quickly as possible, which means dumping it all at the charity shop. What they don't want, the house clearance men will take away.

So we're dead busy and that's OK. Having loads of spare time means you start thinking too much and I've done more than my share of that lately. Sometimes, being here, I've even forgotten about Riley and Skelling in France, at least for a few minutes. (Riley is a boy at school. We were friends. Well, more than friends, I thought for a while, but it's all gone wrong somehow. We used to play guitar together. To be honest, Jupe, Riley's not that good really, but I was trying to help him, passing on all the tips you gave me. And Skelling? Well, she's this girl with highlights who totally hates me. So it's been good for me to get away from all of that.) Anyway, sorting your stuff has been almost fun. But I can't shake off the feeling that there's something else – some reason why you asked us to come to Crickle Cottage.

Am I going crazy? Maybe it's all those creaks in the night. I thought the countryside was supposed to be quiet!

Love,
Clover xxx

Mum and Ed are on something like their ninety-fifth charity shop dash when I spot it, lurking outside in front of the kitchen window. Its fur is straggly and matted and, I have to admit, not unlike mine, pre-Bernice cut.

"Lily!" I yell, pelting outside. "Look who's turned up! It's Jupe's cat. I'm *sure* it's Fuzz."

She thunders towards us. "Oh, isn't he gorgeous?" She reaches out to stroke him, which Fuzz seems perfectly fine with – but when I venture closer he hisses and spits. Yep, that's Fuzz all right.

"Bet no one's feeding him," I say. "Look how skinny he is."

"Let's bring him in," Lily says. We coax him into the kitchen, leaving the front door wide open so he doesn't spark Mum's allergies. Lily rummages through our paltry provisions in Jupe's rust-speckled fridge. We've been here for five days now, existing on basic stuff from the village shop. Ed *still* hasn't caught a fish.

"D'you think he likes ham?" Lily asks.

"Don't know. Let's try him with a little bit." I take out a packet and peel a corner off a slice, placing it on the floor in front of him. Fuzz scoffs it down.

"Wish we could take him home," Lily grumbles, feeding him more ham while stroking his bedraggled fur.

"Mum wouldn't let us," I remind her. "Anyway, he'd probably have Cedric for breakfast."

She sighs and gazes adoringly at him. Fuzz hoovers up the rest of the ham, then pads around the kitchen, sniffing expectantly.

He wanders into the hall, moseying in corners, as if he suspects that Jupe's somewhere in the house, but isn't quite sure where. "Let's see where he goes," I say, quickly shutting Mum and Ed's bedroom door so he doesn't sneak in and strew hairs all over their bed.

He trots upstairs and sniffs in Lily's room, then mine. He prowls up to the top landing, where he looks up and mews. "What does he want?" Lily asks.

I shrug. "No idea."

"Think he's still hungry?"

"He can't be. He's had all our ham. We'll have to tell Mum we ate it in sandwiches, OK?"

Lily nods gravely. Fuzz is really yowling now, all the time straining upwards, stretching his neck, as if he's being pulled up by an invisible thread. I stare up, frowning. There's a hatch up there on the ceiling. The entrance to the attic, probably. "Looks like he wants to go up," I say.

"Maybe that's where he used to sleep," Lily suggests.

"I doubt it. Why would he sleep in the attic? I mean, how would he have got up? Anyway, I'm sure he used to sleep on Jupe's bed."

"Maybe there's something horrible up there," Lily suggests, shuddering, "and only cats can smell it."

"Like what?"

"Like. . ." Her eyes expand so they're almost circular. "Like . . . something *dead*."

"Don't be stupid," I retort. "Look, if you're that worried, let's find a ladder and go up." I shoot her a challenging stare. That'll stop her morbid ideas.

"Yeah," she says brightly. "OK."

"I, um. . ." My heart flips anxiously. "You really want to?"

"Well, *he* does," she says, indicating Fuzz, who's mewing crazily and straining upwards towards the hatch. Like he really is trying to show us something.

"OK," I say firmly. "I'll see if I can find a ladder or something." I check Lily's bedroom, even though I'm pretty sure there's no ladder up here, then hurry down to Mum and Ed's room. It still feels weird. Not Mum and Dad's room, but *Mum and Ed's room*. As if he's become part of our family without us noticing. An old, faded book called *Sea Fishing for Idiots* is plonked on their bed.

There's no ladder there either, or anywhere else in the house. "C'mon," I tell Lily, back on the landing. "If you get on my shoulders, maybe you'll be able to push up the hatch."

"OK," she says eagerly, clambering on to my back as Fuzz yowls and twitches around my ankles.

"It's OK, puss," I say, straightening up so Lily can push the hatch open. Fuzz hisses and turns away in disgust.

It's hard for Lily to lift the hatch at first. She pushes and pushes, jiggling on my shoulders until I'm not sure how much longer I can take the weight of her. "Hurry up," I plead.

"I can't do it, Clover. . ."

"Give it one more try," I tell her. "Quick, they could come back any minute." This time, with an almighty groan, she manages to push the hatch over to one side. Now we can see there's a ladder attached to the opening, which pulls down easily to the floor. I clamber up, with Lily close behind me, relieved that she's the one carrying Fuzz.

The attic smells warm and woody like the inside of a drawer. There's no window, no skylight or anything, so I grope about in the pitch black for a light switch. When I find it, the room fills with dim orangey light. We both peer around as Fuzz springs from Lily's grasp, zooming straight for a scruffy leather armchair. He leaps up and stretches out on it.

I'm staring – not at Fuzz, who I can sense is giving me the evil eye – but at what's laid out before us.

A complete drum kit. A row of guitars lined up on their stands. Amps and mics and chairs all around, crammed into the tiny space. We gawp in silence. It looks as if Jupe and his band could climb the ladder and start playing at any moment. It's his secret room. He never showed us, not even me.

"Wow," Lily breathes. "Why's all this stuff up here?"

"I don't know," I murmur. "Maybe Jupe put it here when the band broke up."

"Why?"

"Lily, I've no idea!" I do, though. Jupe never

admitted he was upset when the band finished. But he was, I could tell. He seemed to miss playing with other people. I sometimes wondered if that's why he enjoyed teaching me so much. "Maybe he just didn't want his bandmates' stuff lying around the house," I add, "because it reminded him of the old days. So I guess he just stuffed it all up here."

"Well," she says, grinning, "aren't you going to play?"

"I . . . I can't, Lily."

"Why not?" she demands.

I pause. It would feel wrong, sort of like trespassing, but how can I tell her that? It would sound crazy.

"Jupe's dead," she reasons. "He wouldn't mind."

I exhale as something catches my eye in the corner. A guitar. Burnt orange, fading to gold in the middle like a sunset. The one I smashed all those years ago.

It's polished and gleaming, as good as new.

I step towards it, wondering now if it really is the same one. But when I'm right up close, I know it is, because it's *not* quite perfect. There's a thin wiggly line where the neck was broken and has been expertly mended. "Go on, play it!" Lily insists, picking up a drumstick and giving the snare drum a gentle tap.

"Shhh!"

"Why? There's no one here. Mum and Ed'll be ages."

"They've only gone to the charity shop," I remind her.

"No," she insists, "they're going fishing as well. They took Jupe's rods."

"Are you sure?"

"Yeah."

Grinning, I eye the guitar on its stand. My hand twitches. I so desperately want to touch it. Just a little go – surely that wouldn't do any harm?

I pick it up and lift the strap over my head. Fuzz glares from his armchair, sending a chill right through me. Slowly, my thumb skims the strings. "Too quiet," Lily announces.

"It's not plugged in, OK? It's supposed to go through an amp."

"Plug it in then." She juts her hands on her hips.

Like it's that simple! I don't know how, because I've never played an electric guitar apart from with Jupe. How long has this stuff been set up for anyway? It could be years since he came up and played. It might be dangerous. What if a billion volts surged through me? I'd be fried to a crisp, and Lily would have to drag me down the ladder and Mum'd go mad.

With an exasperated sigh, Lily plonks herself on the stool behind the drum kit. She picks up a pair of sticks and starts to play. A proper rhythm, I mean, just like that – dead simple. A steady four-four beat. It's not often you're awestruck by your little sister.

"What?" she laughs, stopping.

"That's good!" I say. "How d'you know how to do that?"

She shrugs. "I just do."

"C'mon, someone must have a drum kit and let you have a go. . ."

She's stopped listening because she's playing again, more confidently now, bashing the hell out of the kit. Well, if she's playing, I am too. I find the wall socket, click on the switch and prime myself to be electrocuted – and nothing happens. I'm still alive, at least. I find a lead and, after stabbing it into random sockets, finally strike gold. There's a scream of feedback. Fuzz scoots off his chair, streaks across the floor and cowers behind a speaker in the corner.

I strum quietly, not sure what to play. Then I bang out a chord much louder than I meant to. "That's better!" Lily yelps. I start playing properly, and the first song that pops into my head is "Clover's Song", the one Jupe wrote for me. I haven't figured out how Ed knows it, but playing it now, in Jupe's secret room, it starts to feel like mine again. And it seems right, the two of us playing away. Lily's transfixed by the drums and if Riley was here, it'd almost feel as if we were a band, the three of us. He could sing, I know he could. He's just too shy to give it a try. Lily and I play on, and we're totally lost in the song until there's a bang downstairs and we stop suddenly.

"We're back!" Mum shouts.

I stand dead still. Lily freezes, drumsticks in mid-air.

"Clover? Lily?" Mum yells up. "What's going on up there? Is that you?"

32

Attack of the Killer Moggy

"Clover?" Mum calls again. "Lily? Where *are* you?"

"Upstairs!" I yell back. "We'll be down in a minute."

Pause. "Hurry up, girls. We've got something exciting to show you."

Lily and I stare at each other. "We'll have to get down without them knowing," I hiss.

"Will they be mad, d'you think?" Lily whispers.

"It's not that. You know what Ed's like, always trying to get his hands on Jupe's stuff. He'll want to sell it all, or keep it himself. . ."

"What'll we do with it?" she asks, wide-eyed.

"I don't know! But we'll need to get of here, quick as we can. C'mon, you grab Fuzz – he won't let me touch him." Obediently, she creeps over and tries to pick him up. But he won't let her hold him either. He leaps from her arms, diving under the drum kit and hissing.

"Girls!" Mum bellows.

"We'll have to leave him," I whisper. "One of us can come back and get him as soon as we've spoken to Mum."

"Are you sure. . ." Lily starts.

"What else can we do?" I ask.

"OK," she says, throwing Fuzz an apologetic look. Mum and Ed are chatting away downstairs as we scamper down the ladder and push it back up into place. Lily hops on to my shoulders to replace the hatch, and we pause, catching our breath, on the landing.

"Sure Fuzz'll be OK?" Lily asks, alarmed.

"Hope so. It'll only be a few minutes." I swipe dust from my hair and pray that essence of moggy doesn't seep down through the cracks around the hatch and whoosh straight into Mum's eyes and nostrils. Or, worse, that Fuzz doesn't poop on Jupe's leather chair or pee on all that electric stuff, causing a fizzy explosion so the cottage burns down. What would the landlord say about *that*?

"Promise not to tell Mum or Ed about this, OK?" I remind Lily.

"Promise," she whispers as we head downstairs.

"Hi," I say casually, wandering into the kitchen.

"Hey, girls," Mum says. "What were you two up to upstairs?"

"Just messing about," I say with a shrug.

"Everything all right?" She gives me a quizzical smile.

"Yeah, we're fine. So what've you been doing?"

"Only fishing," she says grandly. "And look what we've got!"

"Ta-*daaa*!" Ed cries, pulling a tea towel off a plate on the table. On the plate is a fish. It's not what you'd call massive. I mean, if we were to have it for lunch, we'd get about half a mouthful each.

"Ed's first catch!" Mum beams.

"It's tiddly," Lily giggles.

"Yeah, but not bad for a beginner," Ed says, sounding hurt.

"It's *fantastic*," Mum gushes, as if he's been out hunting and dragged back a wildebeest, whatever they are, for our lunch. Still, at least cooking it will keep them occupied while I sneak back upstairs and free Fuzz.

Mum rubs her eyes. "I'm feeling a bit scratchy," she says. "There hasn't been a cat in here, has there?"

"Maybe it's Jupe's cat," I suggest quickly. "There's probably still some hairs lying around from when he lived here."

"Funny," she adds. "I've felt fine until now."

"Or perhaps another cat came in through the cat flap," Ed adds.

"I hope not," Mum says with a scowl.

I glance at Lily. You can almost *see* the guilt radiating from her eyeballs.

"Must be the dust, babe," Ed says, gazing proudly at the fish as if it's their newborn baby. I almost expect him to ask, "So, what shall we call it?"

This time, I leave Lily downstairs while I sneak back up to the attic, my heart hammering with fear in case Mum or Ed hear me dragging the chair from my bedroom so I can open up the attic and pull down the ladder by myself. Luckily, they've put the radio on, and everyone's laughing away in the kitchen. Fishy smells start to drift up as they start cooking. I'm so grateful that Fuzz allows himself to be lifted to safety, I could almost kiss him. He winds around my legs as I shut the attic, and obediently follows me downstairs. I tiptoe to the back door, waggle the cat flap and breathe a sigh of relief when he jumps through it.

Lunch is so weird. It reminds me of when you're little and do splodgy paintings at nursery and your parents say, "Oh, that's lovely! Is it a fire engine?" And you're thinking, No, actually, it's a fat red blob where I dropped my paintbrush. And before you know it, it's Blu-Tacked to the fridge above the poetry magnets. Well, that's what it's like with Ed's catch. Mum worked in Tony's chippie for four years, so you wouldn't think it'd be possible for her to get excited about cooking fish. She does, though, because this is

Ed's fish. It's lifted lovingly from an antique frying pan and cut into four tiddly pieces. Amazingly, there's no trumpet fanfare as it's served. Everyone's too polite to ask for a magnifying glass so they can examine their portion.

It takes us about three seconds to eat it, and as we clear the plates, Mum announces that she wants to go out for a walk. "My eyes are still itchy," she adds. "I really need some fresh air."

"Sure," Ed says. "You girls want to come?"

"Um, I'll just stay here," I mutter.

"Me too," Lily says firmly.

Mum shakes her head. "Why on earth d'you want to be cooped up on a gorgeous day like this?"

"You kids," Ed chuckles with a shake of his head. I know he's glad, though, that we're not going. They'll go for a snog on the beach or something, and I don't have the stomach for a freak show right now.

The instant they're gone, me and Lily are out in the garden, hunting around for Fuzz.

"What if he's hungry again?" Lily asks.

"He had all that ham," I remind her, "and Mum's probably right. Cats usually have loads of homes to go to. I bet he's adopted another owner by now and just popped back for a visit. Anyway," I add quickly, "fancy another go on the drums in the attic?"

"Yeah," she enthuses, charging back into the house. "C'mon."

We're giggling hysterically as we pull down the ladder. Then, just as I'm climbing up ahead of Lily, there's a distinct mewing from downstairs. "It's Fuzz!" Lily announces. "Look – he's coming up . . . shall I bring him?"

"Looks like that's what he wants," I laugh as Lily picks up the cat and holds him close to her body as she climbs up after me.

This time, instead of doing her mad-bashing thing, Lily figures out which drum makes which kind of sound and takes it more steadily. And me? Well, I play my own songs, ones I wrote ages ago but have never played to anyone. They feel different and good and I can tell Lily likes them because right away she's picked up the beat.

"Clover," she says as we finish, "what'll happen to all these instruments and stuff?"

My heart slumps. In the excitement of playing, I've been trying to forget the real reason we're here. The landlord wants the house cleared out so he can redecorate and get new tenants in, and it's our job to do it. "I s'pose we'll have to tell Mum and Ed," I tell her. "I mean, we can't just leave it all here."

She swallows hard, her eyes lowered. "Do we have to tell them today?"

"No." I smile at her. "Let's keep it our secret for a bit longer."

"But what'll happen when we *do* tell them?" she demands.

I shrug. "I guess we'll take all the instruments and amps and stuff home in Ed's van. Then. . ." I pause. "Maybe they'll sell it all."

Fuzz springs off his chair and slides past my ankles, his tail twitching irritably.

"Wish we could keep everything," Lily sighs.

"Yeah, me too." I glance around the attic. It should feel spooky – I've spotted huge, hairy spiders – but it's kind of cosy, the way Jupe crammed it with so much stuff all set out and waiting to be found.

Waiting for *us* to find, maybe. The thought sends a chill down my spine. Of course: he stressed that Mum had to sort out his house. *On the condition that you take responsibility for the clearing of Crickle Cottage*, the lawyer said.

And the only person in our family who'd be thrilled to discover the sunset guitar would be . . . me.

I glance at Lily, who's tapping a gentle rhythm on the snare. Maybe Jupe knew I'd find it. Perhaps that's why he brought us here – so I'd see that the sunset guitar was mended and almost perfect again.

Maybe he wanted to say sorry for the row, for us all storming off, for never getting in touch or even answering any of my letters.

A lump clogs my throat. I start to strum, and try to sing, but the words come out all knotted up. "We'd better get down," I say quickly, "in case they come back. C'mon, let's get Fuzz."

"Let's stay a bit longer," Lily whines.

"No, we can't risk it, OK?"

She throws down the drumsticks, grumbling in frustration as I lift Fuzz from Jupe's chair. Or rather, *try* to lift, as he thrashes out, slicing into my wrist with his claws and flying across the floor in a furious blur. "Ow!" I yelp as blood springs from the gash.

"What happened?" Lily exclaims.

"He scratched me!"

She lurches over. "You're bleeding! What'll you tell Mum?"

"Nothing," I say firmly. "Hopefully, she won't even notice." I pull down my sleeve, which is immediately splodged with bright crimson. My wrist is already stinging like blazes.

I'm wrong, too, about Mum not noticing. "Oh, Clover," she cries later, swooping on me when she spots the tatty bandage I made from a strip of pillowcase. "What on earth have you done?"

"Nothing," I fib. "Just scratched it when I was out playing with Lily."

"Why didn't you say?" she cries. "Here, let's take that horrible bandage off, make sure it's not dirty or anything." Obediently, I let her unwind the material, wash it thoroughly under the tap and pat it dry. "It's pretty nasty," she adds. "Are you sure it's not really hurting?"

I shake my head firmly. "It's fine, Mum, honestly." Which only counts as a tiny lie, doesn't it?

33

Gold Leather Trousers

The next few days slide by in a blur of swimming at Silver Cove, and sneaking up to Jupe's den whenever we get the chance. So far, apart from his solitary fish, Ed's only managed to catch seaweed and ripped polythene with Jupe's rods, and I've tried to swivel my gaze in the opposite direction when he's strutted through the cottage in his glossy second-skin trunks.

I spend evenings poring over Jupe's old newspaper interviews, hoping to find out why it happened. The row, I mean. The falling-out-with-us-for-ever thing, despite him apparently *doting* on his little musical niece. I call Dad, hoping he'll explain what went on after the car crash. "Your mum was so upset and angry," he says, "she made it absolutely clear she never wanted any contact with him again." I don't ask why he thinks Jupe never replied to my letters. Mum and Dad didn't even know I'd sent them, and I'd feel stupid telling him now. Sometimes, when I'm engrossed in one of Jupe's newspaper interviews, I start playing that game again, where it's *me* being interviewed. Me, Clover Jones, with the scabby wrist, which is now covered up with a fresh bandage applied by Mum.

The interview starts really well.

So, Clover, congratulations on the new album. I have to say it's a move on from anything you've done before.
Thanks. I'm really pleased with it.
A solo effort too. That's some achievement. . .
It was easier in a way. No one to please but myself. And I found that—
But can I just ask. . . (Interviewer butts in rudely.)
Er, as I was saying. . .
It must be awful for you, with this brilliant album – yet it's Riley who's on the sell-out tour and all the magazine covers. . .
Um, yeah, well, me and Riley sort of went off in separate ways. He was doing all that cheesy girlie stuff – I mean poppy *stuff – with Sophie Skelling, which is great and everything, but really wasn't my thing, cough, splutter. . .* (Interviewer is looking at me very oddly. I suspect he'll write: "At this point, Clover turns a very strange sickly colour and is clearly completely heartbroken. . .")

And of course, they've been hugely successful. . .

Yes, and I'm really, really pleased for them. Him. Er, I mean. . . (Teeth firmly gritted.)

All the same, Clover, don't you feel a tiny bit jealous that they're selling out huge venues and are about to embark on a world tour?

Of course I'm not jealous! Why would I be? I'm completely delighted for them! (Voice rises, verging on hysteria.)

And rumour has it that you were really close to Riley. . .

I'd really appreciate it if we didn't turn this interview into the Riley Hart show, OK?

OK, sorry. Just one more question. Were you and Riley ever more than just. . . Ah. Looks like our interview's over. Clover Jones has left the building.

On our second to last day at Jupe's, I find them. The gold leather trousers, neatly folded at the back of his wardrobe. They're all cracked and wrinkly like an old lady's handbag you'd find at a jumble sale. "God, were they really in there?" Mum laughs, shaking her head. "I was sure I'd cleaned it out. I packed up the rest of his clothes for charity a few days ago."

"Yeah, we could've made a fortune out of those band T-shirts," Ed grumbles.

"They were ripped," Mum protests, "and smelly."

"All the better!" Ed declares. "That was genuine Jupe sweat."

"Well, these aren't going anywhere," I say, gripping the trousers.

"Hey, let me try 'em on," Ed guffaws, trying to snatch them from me.

"No!" I squeal.

"What are *you* going to do with them, Clover?" Mum asks.

"I don't know." I shrug. "Just keep them, I guess."

She smiles. "OK. I s'pose you'll want a little memento. . ."

"Can we keep more stuff?" I blurt out.

She squints at me. "Like what? Just about everything's gone, love. We don't have the space anyway, and I'm not keen on filling up our house with clutter. . ."

My insides slump. Nothing guitar-shaped then. Or as huge and unwieldy as a drum kit. Lily glances up from the kitchen table where she's been drawing, and I'm shocked at how upset she looks. I'd always assumed nothing really bothered her – not even Dad leaving – as long as she can still go to Brownies and chocolate fountain parties.

"Clover," Mum says suddenly, "hasn't your wrist healed yet? Here, let me see. . ."

"It's fine," I say quickly.

"Come on, let me check." She removes the bandage and examines the scabby red lines. "This *isn't* fine, Clover . . . it's still quite nasty." She frowns at me, and my heart starts to thud. "It looks like something scratched you," she adds.

"It was, um. . ." I pause a beat too long. "It was just a stray cat prowling about outside."

"So why did you lie?" she exclaims.

"I just, um . . . didn't want to make a fuss."

Sighing, Mum hugs me to her chest. "Don't keep secrets, love. If something's hurt you, I want to know about it, OK?"

I focus on the dull orange kitchen floor. "Yeah, I know." What, like the fact that the attic's stuffed with instruments that we can't take home – because she can't be doing with clutter? And besides, if Ed was excited about finding Jupe's stinky old T-shirts, how would we stop him selling a load of guitars?

Jupe wanted me to find the sunset guitar. I just know it. And it's up to me to keep it safe.

On our last day in Cornwall, Lily and I go for a swim while Ed messes about with Jupe's fishing rods. By the time we head back, leaving Ed cursing on the rocks, Mum's pretty much packed up. Crickle Cottage looks strange and empty. Mum still hasn't ventured up into the attic. Maybe she hasn't even noticed the hatch. It's not as if any of us even went up there when Jupe was alive.

"Hi, girls," she says as we wander into the kitchen. I can tell she's putting on a brave face. "You'd better start packing up your things. We'll be leaving after dinner."

"Um . . . do we have to?" I ask.

She pulls a tight smile. "Of course we do, sweetheart. Nothing to stay for now, is there?"

"*Miaow!*" Fuzz appears in the doorway.

"What's that cat doing in here?" Mum cries. "Did one of you leave the front door open?"

"Don't think so," I start.

Mum marches towards him, then stops and stares. "Is it Jupe's cat?"

"Erm, I don't know," comes my tiddly voice.

Fuzz arches his back and hisses. "It is, isn't it?" Mum declares. "Is this the cat that scratched you?"

"Um, I'm not sure. . ." I babble.

"*Is* it Fuzz?" She turns to Lily, who blushes furiously.

"Er. . ." Lily croaks.

"Yes, it is," I say miserably. "What'll we do, Mum? He was just prowling around outside, all skinny and miserable looking. . ."

"Is that what's been happening to our bits and pieces from the fridge?" she demands.

I nod bleakly. "We can't leave him here. He's got nowhere to go."

"Well," Mum says, sniffing, "I'm sorry, love, but we can't keep him either. . ."

The front door flies open, and Fuzz scampers out. "Hey," Ed says on the doorstep, "whose cat is that?"

"It's Jupe's," Mum says, shaking her head, "and it clawed Clover's hand to shreds."

Ed tuts loudly. "What'll we do with him?"

"I don't know, Ed," she retorts. "I've got enough to think about at the moment. . ."

"Hey, listen," he says gently, "it's our last supper, OK? I'm going to cook a surprise."

"That'd be great," Mum says wearily, "but what are you cooking?"

"Come and see." We all cluster around him as, grinning, he opens his canvas fishing bag – correction, *Jupe's* fishing bag; he's probably going to try and flog that too – on the kitchen table and pulls out a newspaper parcel. Unwrapping it slowly, he holds out his prize.

It's a huge fish, glinting silver as if it's been daubed with Lily's glitter glue. "That's fantastic, Ed," Mum says, her voice wobbling with emotion. He plonks his catch on the table and pulls her towards him with his stinky-fish hands. "What's wrong, love?" he asks gently.

"Oh, Ed," Mum says, crying now, "it's been awful today, doing the last of the packing up. It just feels so . . . final, that's all." I stare, feeling helpless. There's a horrible choking sob as Mum clings to Ed.

"Shhh, Kerry. . ." He buries his round, shiny face in her hair. "It had to be done and you've been so brave. . ."

I glance at Lily, who's gnawing fretfully on a

fingernail. "Mum," I venture cautiously, "if, um, there was anything else of Jupe's in the house, couldn't we just take it home?"

"What, like Fuzz?" she asks wearily.

"No, I mean, er, other things," I blurt out.

She gives me a faint smile. "I'm sorry, Clover. Everything's gone. Now, if Ed starts cooking, you girls can set the table. . ." She glances up, and there's a black blur as Fuzz leaps from a chair to the table, then streaks for the kitchen door, Ed's fish clamped firmly in his mouth.

"Damn cat!" Ed roars, flying out after him. As Mum tears out too, and the pair of them charge across the scrubby ground, Lily and I collapse in helpless, teary laughter.

Last Song at Jupe's

Ed can't contemplate driving home on an empty stomach, so he and Mum have driven to the village to fetch fish and chips for dinner. Which leaves me and Lily alone in the house.

Our last chance. Thanks, Fuzz – we owe you one.

The instant they're gone, we're zooming up to the attic. "What shall we play?" Lily asks, brandishing her drumsticks impatiently (they've become *her* drumsticks).

"I don't know," I say. There isn't much time. We'll only manage one song, so it feels important to get it right.

"What about that one Jupe wrote for you?" she asks.

I push away the image of Ed playing "Clover's Song" with his eyes screwed up, refusing to tell me how he knew it. "OK," I say, picking up the sunset guitar. "Think you can remember it?"

"Of course," she says, laughing. Then she's playing the intro, and I'm straight in, and it's as if Jupe's here with us, insisting that we *could* be a real band, even though I'm no singer – even he'd admit that. But we could find one, couldn't we? And a bass player too? What was it he said about finding your soulmates? Jupe always believed I'd make something of myself. And I promised I'd give it my best shot, didn't I?

"Let's play it again," I say recklessly. And we do, over and over, until the song's sounding almost right. We try playing it faster, then slow it right down, not noticing time ticking away, and no longer caring that Mum and Ed could come back with our fish and chips any minute. . .

"Well, look what we've got here!"

I stop dead. Lily staggers to a halt on the drums. My eyes slide in the direction of the open hatch.

And I try to speak, but no words come out. A round, pink head has popped up through the hatch, its raisiny eyes fixed upon us. "So," Ed says with a slow smile. "*This* is what you've been up to."

He steps up through the hatch. I've frozen with the sunset guitar slung across my body.

"Can't believe it," Ed gasps, gazing around in wonder. "This must be Jupe's band stuff. It's incredible." He walks around slowly, touching each instrument in turn. I can't move, can't even look at Lily. "Why didn't you say anything about this?" he asks.

I sense Lily staring at me, willing me to speak, to be the big sister who always knows what to do. Ha! When have I ever been good at that? "We . . . just wanted it to be our thing," I mumble. "We, um. . ." I know how feeble this'll sound. "We were . . . pretending to be in a real band," I add meekly.

A smile spreads over Ed's face. It's a kind smile, which softens his eyes, crinkling their corners. "Well, I can understand that," he says. "It's like a shrine, isn't it, to your uncle?"

I nod, speechless.

"Ed!" Mum cries, and I hear her trotting lightly upstairs. "Where are you? The fish and chips are getting cold."

"We're in the attic," Ed calls back.

"Why? What are you doing up there?"

"Come and see," Ed calls back. "You won't believe it, Kerry."

"What's going on?" Her voice is coming from the landing now. There's the faintest smell of vinegary fish and chips.

"Not sure I fancy climbing that rickety old ladder," Mum announces. "It doesn't look safe, Ed, and I'm not great with heights. . ."

"You'll be fine," he says, stepping down to help her. "Just take it slowly, OK? You're not going to fall."

"I really don't like ladders," she protests.

"C'mon, you have to see this!"

"All right, Ed," Mum replies. "Don't rush me. . ." I can hear the ladder's metallic creaks, then her face appears at the hatch, eyes widening as she takes in the scene. "My God," she breathes. "So he did keep everything after all. Why on earth didn't you tell us, girls?"

"We, um, were just . . . playing," Lily whispers.

I take off the guitar and carefully place it on its stand. Mum stares at it. "That's not . . . the one, is it? The one you dropped?"

"Yes," I say dully.

Mum steps towards it and runs a fingertip across its smooth surface. "Are you sure, darling?"

"Uh-huh."

"It's as good as new," she says in a whisper. "I tried to tell him it could be fixed, but he kept saying that wasn't the point, that it would never be the same again. . ." My heart feels like it's being squeezed like a lemon. "He was wrong, wasn't he, Clover?" she adds.

"Guess so," I say. Here it comes: *How much d'you think we'll get for all this stuff? Maybe enough to have that cruddy back porch knocked down that your dad should never have built in the first place, and a proper extension put up, or a home gym for Ed, for when he moves in and becomes your new stepdad. . . Oh my God, Ed, we're going to be rich!*

I stare at Mum, barely able to breathe. It's Ed who breaks the silence. "So, Kerry, bet you didn't know your Lily's one hell of a drummer?"

We pick at cold, clammy fish and chips, have a final check of the house and post the keys through the letter box at the solicitor's office. Then we drive home in Ed's van. I catch a last glimpse of Silver Cove, the sea glinting in the distance.

There's a song playing in my head that no one else can hear. It's the one Jupe wrote for me. It's gentler than his other songs, which makes it seem even more special. Most of Jupe's fans would be surprised to hear it, but I always knew there was another, softer side to him.

A bit like with Mum, who's looking out at the green, rolling hills and faraway sliver of sea. On my other side is Lily, and on her lap is a wicker basket. And inside that basket is a slight less scrawny but still mean-tempered ball of black fur called Fuzz.

35

Home Sweet Home

It's after eleven when we get home. Mum carries a sleeping Lily up to bed, and even tucks me in, as if I'm little again too. "We'll unpack the van in the morning," she says. "Ed's too tired to do it now."

I nod, feeling bleary after three hours in the van. "What are we going to do with all Jupe's stuff?" I whisper.

She's silent for a moment, and perches lightly on the edge of my bed. "We can't keep it, love."

I nod, feeling a lump tightening in my throat. "I knew you'd say that."

"It's the space, and it'd be far too noisy," she adds gently, but I wonder if that's all it is. Maybe she just doesn't want reminders of Jupe lying around our house. Kissing my forehead, Mum gets up to leave. "I'm sorry, Clover," she says as she closes the bedroom door.

Jess is round at our house by nine-thirty next morning, brown as a berry from her holiday. "What's all this stuff?"

she asks as we haul out guitars, amps and drums from the back of Ed's van.

"My uncle's instruments," I explain. "We found them all hidden away in the attic."

"Wow," she breathes. "What are you going to do with them all, though? I mean, how many guitars d'you need?"

Just two, I think: my own acoustic, and the sunset one. "We're selling them," I say, keeping my voice perky.

"Course we are," Mum says, lifting the drum stool from the van. "We can't have electric guitars and drums in a terraced house. You do understand that, don't you, darling?"

"Suppose so," I mumble.

"Jupe lived in the middle of nowhere," Mum adds, turning to Jess. "He could make as much noise as he liked. . ." She laughs, but it sounds forced and uncomfortable.

"If I could keep the drums," Lily grumbles, staring at the pavement, "I wouldn't have any birthday or Christmas presents for years and years."

"Hon, I've explained," Mum says wearily, "virtually all the way home, with my nose streaming from that cat . . . just drop it, would you, please?"

Lily scowls. "I only said. . ."

Jess shuffles uncomfortably on our front path. "C'mon," I tell her, "let's go round and see Betty and show her Fuzz. We're going to ask if she wants to adopt him."

"Think she will?" Lily asks.

"Hope so," I say, grinning. I'm proud of my sister for not stropping about Fuzz. She knows Mum's allergic, and that him living next door might be the next best thing to having a cat of her own. Anyway, he's always made it pretty clear he doesn't like me. Maybe he was jealous because Jupe made such a fuss of me when I was younger. If that's the case, cats don't half bear a grudge.

As Jess, Lily and I head around to Betty's, I figure that I don't really mind about selling the other guitars. It's only the sunset one I want to keep – plus the amps and mics and drum kit for Lily – but I've given up wishing and hoping.

I did all that with Riley, and where did that get me?

36

Skelling's Return

Our "holiday" seems to have fired up Mum. During our first week back she has three job interviews, and by the following week she's been offered a job at the travel agent's next to Pet Heaven. "Well done, sweetheart," Ed says, grinning approvingly as she models her sky blue skirt and blouse, blue high heels and spotted tie.

I have to hold in a bubble of laughter – not because it doesn't suit her, but because she looks totally respectable and not like my mum at all. The company's motto, which is embroidered on the blouse pocket, reads: *Reaching for the skies*, which I suppose is a slight improvement on *Smiles cost nothing so we give them for free*, which Tony put on the wall at the chip shop and which would be harder to fit on to a pocket, I guess.

The brilliant thing is, she hasn't had time to do anything about selling Jupe's guitars and drum kit yet. She's been too busy doing herself up to start the job – including, at this precise moment, having her hair done at (eek!) the Cutting Room because Drunk Babs is on holiday. "You can't go there," I blurted out before she set off for her Thursday morning appointment.

"Why not?" she laughed. "*You* go, don't you?"

"Well, just the once. . ." I could feel myself blushing furiously.

"So what's the problem?" Mum asked.

I opened and closed my mouth, my heart juddering as I wondered whether to blurt out the truth. "Um . . . Bernice works there," I said in a whisper.

Mum stepped back and frowned at me, as if she was about to give me an almighty lecture about keeping this from her. "So what?" she said with an exaggerated shrug. "I'll go where I like to have my hair cut. *I've* nothing to be embarrassed about, have I? I mean, I don't have people drawing me with my clothes off." And off she went, as if almost looking forward to breezing into the salon and freaking out Bernice.

It's so nerve-shredding, thinking of Mum confronting Bernice in the salon, that all I can do is plug in Jupe's sunset guitar and play and play, while Lily bashes the hell out of the drums that Ed set up temporarily in our room.

Can you believe that Mum actually complained about Lily's drumming? "But you love music!" my sister protested. "You play it really loud. . ."

"That's different," Mum argued.

"Why? How's it different?"

"Because," she said with a toss of her hair, "you can turn my music off."

Which, admittedly, you can't do with Lily Jones.

It feels like Mum's been at the Cutting Room for a hundred years. Lily's out too, having rushed off to help with a Brownie fundraising stall on the seafront. I check the street from my bedroom window to see if Mum's storming up the road after a huge row with Bernice. I *hope* there's not been any violence. Then I see him: Riley Hart. My ex-friend, who's supposed to be in France right now. Maybe they've all come back early. Or they could have had a furious row on holiday, and his dad had to rush out to collect him. . . I watch him, trying to will him to cross the road and knock at my door.

He glances at our house and I stagger back from my bedroom window, sensing my cheeks flaming up. Not that he's looking at *our* house, of course, so there's no danger of him seeing me. He's walking self-consciously, as if it's taking all his effort *not* to look, then he marches round the corner out of sight.

Well, I'm not having that. The cheek of it! He can't stroll down my street, where I've lived *all my life*, trying to make me feel bad. My hands are all sweaty and I can tell I've gone blotchy in the face. Why do bodies behave like this? You read in magazines that when you see someone you like, these amazing things happen to make you appear more attractive so that person will fall in love with you. Your lips are supposed to plump up and go pinker and your pupils are meant to turn into huge black saucers so you look totally gorgeous.

I examine my face in our mirror. While my cheeks are sizzling, my lips are washed out, barely visible. My pupils are tiny pinpricks. If anything, I look sick.

I put the sunset guitar away in its scruffy case, place it on my bed and hurry downstairs. Then I grab my keys and head out.

I'm not actually going to Riley's house. I just seem to swerve in that direction, carried along by my legs with no say in where they're taking me. Soon his house is in view. It's a muggy afternoon filled with cooking smells. I want to turn back but my legs won't let me. Now I'm outside his place, and I can sense that my pupils are as tiny as it's possible to be. Because, you see, I don't even *like* him any more. I don't even want to see him. It's just . . . I need to know why he isn't in France, what's going on with him and Skelling, why he didn't seem to care about cutting me out of his life, just like Jupe did. Then, once I know, I can forget all about him and be normal again, like I was before Riley came to Copper Beach.

My mouth's dry and my tongue feels like a shrivelled-up Jurassic burger as I knock firmly on his front door.

*

For a few seconds, no one answers. Maybe he's not in. He was probably just passing my house on his way down to the North Cove or something. Then, just as I'm about to turn back, there are soft footsteps in the hall, and the door opens slowly.

"Hi," Riley says, looking surprised. "You all right?"

"Er, yeah. I . . . I was just passing," I start, "and I wondered, I mean. . . I didn't think you'd be back from holiday yet. From, er, France," I add dumbly.

He looks at me and blinks. "So why did you come?" he asks.

"I, um. . ." Now I'm trapped. Well done, Clover, idiot. "I saw you in our street," I add lamely, "and I wondered if, er . . . anyway." We stare at each other. "Did you have a good time?" I blurt out.

"No, I didn't," he says coolly.

"Oh." I'm starting to sweat now. Nice. "So, er . . . what happened?"

"I didn't have a good time," he says slowly, "because I didn't go."

He didn't go! He didn't go! "Why not?" I ask.

Riley shrugs. "I just didn't, OK? Plans changed."

I nod, and a tiny spark of hope bursts like a firework in my heart. *He didn't go! He didn't go!* I'm grinning crazily and I don't care.

There was no slathering sunscreen on to Skelling's bare-naked skin.

No drooling over custard bikinis.

No kissing by the pool in the moonlight.

"Well," I say, trying to normalize my expression, "I'm back from my uncle's now, er, as you can see . . . and he died, did I tell you that? And he, er, left us everything, so we've brought back all these instruments. . ."

"Yeah?" Riley says icily.

"I . . . I thought you might want to come over. And, um, see them. And play. . ." Why am I asking him over? This isn't what I planned to say at all. I was going to be brave and straight to the point. I open my mouth, but can't think of anything else to say.

He pretends to swipe an insect from his brown, beautiful neck. "Clover," he mutters, "I don't want to do music with you any more."

Crash, goes my heart. Like Lily thrashing Jupe's cymbal. "But . . . why not?"

His eyes are cold and hard. "Well, I didn't think *you* would after that time you stomped off. . ."

"I just wanted to know about Sophie and—" I start.

"Anyway," he cuts in angrily, "why should I hang out with you after what you've been saying about me?"

"What? But I haven't said anything!"

"Don't lie," he snaps. "I know what you've said. That I'm crap at playing guitar, and it's so embarrassing when I come round, and you only spend time with me 'cause you feel sorry for me, but really you wish I'd jack it in and save you the trouble of humouring me. . ."

He's yelling now, really yelling. A woman pulling a

shopping basket on wheels stares at us from across the street.

"I didn't say that!" I yell back. "I've never said *anything* like that. Who told you?"

His mouth forms a grim line. How can such a sweet, handsome face look so brittle? "Doesn't matter," he says airily.

"Yes, it does," I shout, "because they're lying!"

He folds his arms. "No, they're not."

"How d'you know? How can you be so sure?"

"Because," he starts, glancing down at his grubby trainers, "everyone knows you're a brilliant guitarist. And when I thought about it – all those hours you've spent trying to help me, when I've played the same thing over and over and *still* couldn't get it. . ." He snorts. "No one would do that without getting frustrated."

My eyes flood with tears. I'd give anything for some kind of Hoover thingie behind my eyeballs to suck them back in. They wobble like mercury on my lower lids and then – dammit – overflow and drip down my cheeks. "You really believe that?" I ask, my voice splintering.

Riley shrugs. "I don't see any reason not to."

Furiously, I swipe my tears with a sleeve. "Why didn't you go to France, Riley? What happened?"

He sighs deeply. "At first I said I'd go," he mutters, " 'cause me and Dad never go on holiday. We haven't been anywhere since Mum left. But then, when I thought about it – being away for the whole summer – I realized I wanted to be here. With you."

"With . . . *me*?" I croak.

Riley nods.

I swallow hard. He chose boring old Copper Beach over France, because of me? "You mean," I venture, "even though I'm supposed to have said those horrible things about you?"

"By the time I heard all that, it was too late to go 'cause they'd already booked their flights."

"Right. So . . . Skelling told you that stuff, did she?"

He shuffles on the doorstep. "It doesn't matter," he mumbles.

"Who was it, Riley?" I'm not crying any more. I'm just mad, mad as hell.

"Just someone, OK?"

"And you don't think that *someone* was jealous of all the time we'd been spending together?"

He opens his mouth to speak. For a moment, he looks as if he realizes it's a horrible, tangled mess, but that it's too late to unravel it.

"Hey, Riley!" come a shrill voice from upstairs. "I thought you were going to play that song for me? Who are you talking to down there?"

There are footsteps, the clack-clack of heels on the wooden staircase. "Oh, hi, Clover!" Skelling exclaims. She's wearing teeny white shorts and a bubblegum-pink lacy vest.

"What are you doing here?" I blurt out.

She flashes a syrupy smile. "Had to come back early. Dad was offered this amazing job he couldn't turn down. He's getting a company car and everything."

"Just a car?" I ask coldly. "Not a yacht or a helicopter?" Whoops, that popped right out of my mouth.

She snorts, pony-like, through her nostrils. "Anyway, what were you were saying to Riley? That I'm *jealous* of you? Why would I be jealous when you're the one who lives in a scabby house, whose dad's gone off with some naked model and a mum who—"

"Hey!" Riley cuts in. "No need to—"

"Jealous of your holiday, maybe?" she crows. "I mean, we only went to dreary old France, while you . . . you went to a dead man's house, didn't you?" She throws back her head and guffaws.

"Sophie, for God's sake," Riley snaps, whirling round to face her. "That's . . . that's a horrible thing to say. . ."

She rolls her eyes and simpers. "Sorry."

"No," he says, shooting her a furious look. "Don't speak to Clover like that. You don't know *anything* about her." Riley's cheeks are burning and even Skelling has the decency to turn a hot shade of pink.

"Of course you're not jealous of me," I snap at her. "Why would you be? You've got everything." I turn and storm away, shutting my ears as Riley shouts out my name, his voice fading to nothing as I run.

★

You're welcome to each other, I fume as I charge home. *I hope you'll be deliriously happy together.* It's not as if Riley's ever been my boyfriend or my anything at all. Guitar practice, that's all it was. Someone to try out new songs with, to see if they worked, because it's awfully lonely playing all by yourself.

So really, Riley could have been *anybody.*

And he's right – he never gets any better. His strings buzz and he drops his plectrum and gets frustrated and red in the face. Sometimes I wonder why he persists with lessons at Niall's. Maybe his dad pushes him into it.

Oh yeah, and there were those kisses. The tiny, blink-and-you'd-miss-it kiss, and the real one. Well, a girl can make mistakes. For a moment just then, I actually thought he was, you know, OK after all. Especially when he said he wanted to stay at Copper Beach instead of going to France. Now I know better. Even if he likes me, Skelling's always going to be around, trying to ruin my life. I'm not having that any more. I'd rather spend my time washing all the panes in Dad's greenhouse than hang out with him. I'd rather clean Cedric's cage with my tongue.

By the time I turn into our road, I've come up with some new rules for myself:

1. Remember my promise to Jupe. Get better and better on guitar, find a band, rehearse until we're

completely brilliant and make Riley Hart completely, sickly jealous. Ha!

2. And, er, that's it. I can't think of anything else. But it's big enough to be going on with, don't you think? And it's working already because it's taken my mind off Riley for . . . ooh, about seventeen seconds.

Mum's New Do

Mum comes home from the Cutting Room with her crinkly, purplish Drunk-Babs mane transformed into a glossy chestnut bob. She looks gorgeous, like a model.

"It looks great, Mum," I enthuse, hoping to God that this was Bernice's day off.

"Think so?" she asks, grinning. "It's a big change. . ."

"Yeah, but it suits you."

"She was really persuasive," Mum adds, twirling a strand of hair with a finger.

"Who?" I ask shakily.

"The hairdresser." A sly smile flickers across her lips. "The one who did such a lovely job with *your* hair, remember?"

It feels like flames are whooshing up my face. After Riley today, I'm not sure how much more stress I can take. "Mum, I—" I start, but she comes over and hugs me. Her hair feels soft and smells of coconut.

"It's OK," she murmurs. "You already told me

Bernice works there, and I'm glad you warned me. But you never told me she'd actually cut your hair, did you?" I shake my head. "Well," Mum adds, "she let it slip, because she ended up cutting mine too."

"Er, was that OK?" I ask nervously.

Mum smiles. "Sort of. We figured out who each other was, and of course it was awkward – but, you know, it was kind of funny too."

"Funny?" I repeat faintly.

"Well, our paths were going to cross one day. And you can hardly start ranting at someone who's cutting your hair, can you? God knows what they'd do with their scissors. . ."

I manage a weak laugh, and all the knotted ropes in my stomach start to loosen.

"Listen, Clover," Mum adds, "your dad and me . . . well, things weren't right for years. I don't think we'd been happy for a long time." She turns away and drops two tea bags into mugs.

"And, um . . . are you happy now?" I ask.

She looks over her shoulder and grins. "Yes, I really am. That week at Jupe's helped me realize that. I felt . . . really close to Ed there."

I nod, not knowing what to say.

"In fact," she adds, "I was thinking of asking if he'd like to move in with us, if that would be all right with you. . ."

"What, here?" I squeak. "In our house?"

She nods, handing me a steaming mug. "I know it's a bit quick, but he's living in a tiny rented flat and his landlord's told him that he's thinking of selling the place. So you see, love, he might have nowhere else to go." She fixes me with her slate grey eyes. "I hope you're OK with this, sweetheart. If you're not, I won't mention it to him."

Am I OK? I haven't the faintest idea *what* I am. All these things have happened – Jupe dying, Dad meeting Bernice, Mum falling in love with Ed, Riley deciding that I'm the most despicable thing on earth and that he'd rather believe the lies of a total airhead. How am I supposed to know what's OK? "It's up to you, Mum," I say firmly.

"Well, I don't want it to happen if you're going to be unhappy. . ."

I take a deep breath. It feels disloyal to Dad, but then, he's not coming back, is he? And was it really so bad, having Ed around at Jupe's? "It's OK," I say.

"Really?" Her eyes are shining as she throws her arms around me. "I'm really glad, Clover. And you know what? I'm so proud of you."

I smile and step back, looking at new-look Mum who's just had her hair done by Dad's girlfriend. And I guess I'm proud of her too.

38

Guitars for Sale

A week later, Ed's sort of moved in already. His toothbrush has arrived at least, and some nights he stays over. It's weird getting used to Ed being in my life so much, and Riley not being in it at all. It's tempting to go round to his place and try to explain that I didn't say that stuff, but what would be the point? A girl's got to have pride. At least Niall's guitar lessons stop during the summer holidays, so I won't have to deal with Riley being all cold and distant with me until the start of term. And by then, I'll be over him, won't I?

Anyway, there's other stuff going on that's far more worrying than a stupid boy with a Skelling obsession. One scorching-hot day I come back from hanging out with Jess at the beach to find a man with a bushy grey moustache in our living room. He's wearing biker's leathers and is examining Jupe's guitars, having phoned about the ad that Mum put in the paper. At first he didn't believe they were Jupe's. "I'm his sister," I heard

Mum explaining on the phone. "I've got photos, newspaper cuttings, where you can clearly see what he was playing. Yes, they're all for sale. . ."

A pause, where Mum rolled her eyes. "Uh-huh . . . yes, I know that doesn't prove they're the *actual ones*," she went on, "but you'll just have to trust me, OK? Otherwise, don't bother coming."

He's here now, peering suspiciously around our living room, as if we might have more of Jupe's stuff lurking in corners. Of course, the rest of his belongings went to charity, or were left for the clearance men to take away, as Mum couldn't face sifting through every single little thing. "OK if I try them all out?" he asks.

"Of course," Mum says brightly. "Take your time. Clover and Ed will answer any questions, won't you, guys? I'll leave you to it." She hurries away to the kitchen.

Ed nods, sipping from a bottle of sports drink, and I fidget in the corner of the room. I wish I wasn't here. I'd rather be at Dinosaur Diner than here. The man picks up a pale blue guitar and whacks out a chord. "Needs tuning," he complains, but that doesn't put him off playing some more. He perches on the sofa arm, attempting a showy solo, his eyes squeezed tightly shut.

I trap a laugh. Ed catches my eye and grins. The giggle forms deep in my belly, and I have to think about bad things – like Skelling yelling at me from Riley's front door – to stop myself convulsing. "Nah," the man says. "I'm looking for something with a deeper, rounder sound, y'know?" He glances around, and his eyes light upon the sunset guitar.

No, I think desperately. *You don't want that one. It doesn't have the deep, round sound you're looking for.*

He scratches his scalp. "You say you've got a drum kit?"

Lily, who's been sulking upstairs, comes down and peeps into the living room. "It's upstairs," Ed says, "in the girls' room. I'll show you if you like."

Lily throws me a horrified look. "I wouldn't bother looking at it, though," Ed adds quickly. "Pile of rubbish, that is. Virtually falling to bits. Unplayable."

"I might just have a look," the man says. He stands up, and his leather trousers creak ominously.

"Nah, mate," Ed insists, "I can tell you're serious, yeah? Looking for quality gear? Honestly, you wouldn't let a little kid loose on that kit. In fact, I don't think anyone in Jupe's band ever played it."

Shrugging, the man plods over to inspect the sunset guitar. Lily's staring at me, aghast. "That's twenty grand," Ed says coolly.

"What?" the man gasps. "Your ad didn't say that!"

"Yeah, but that one's not part of the ad," Ed says firmly. "It's special, mate, and we're not taking any offers."

I have to bite my lip to stop myself from grinning.

"Aw, come on. . ." The man reaches out to pick it up.

"I said *no offers*," Ed says sharply, and the man jerks his hand away.

He glowers at us, shaking his head. "Your ad was misleading, then."

"Take it or leave it," Ed says with a shrug.

Sighing, the man delves into a jacket pocket and pulls out a wad of banknotes. He flicks through them, mouthing the numbers. "There," he says, handing the money to Ed and nodding towards the blue guitar. "I'll take that one."

"Great," Ed says, smiling.

"It's gonna need an overhaul," the man huffs, giving my sunset guitar a lingering glance as he leaves.

Whoops, see what I did? I said *my* sunset guitar.

What happens the next day is even weirder. A bunch of people come around – one painfully shy man, who shuffles away with a cheap, battered black guitar, and a witchy woman with black-rimmed eyes who has the girliest voice imaginable. "I'm interested in this," she says, plucking the sunset guitar's strings.

"Twenty grand," Ed says firmly. As she's busy with her new job at the travel agent's, Mum has appointed Ed as the Responsible Adult (ha!) to oversee the proceedings. I suspect, though, that she doesn't want to see Jupe's stuff being taken away. I mean, it's not like leaving his lumpy old beds and tatty wardrobes for the clearance men. Even Mum knows instruments are different.

The third person insists on trying out the drums, and eventually Ed gives in and takes him up to our room. "Nice kit," the man says. "I'm looking for something like this for my daughter." Lily, who's in an almighty black mood, has mooched off to play with Fuzz round at Betty's.

"Look, mate," Ed says, "I'm really sorry, but I'm in an awkward position. You see, someone came round earlier and put a deposit on the drums, so I'm not really at liberty to sell."

"Did they?" I blurt out, and Ed wiggles his eyebrows at me.

"Why didn't you say?" the man asks, tapping the cymbal irritably.

"Well, um, I thought I'd let you try 'em out in case this other sale falls through. . ."

The man hisses between his teeth. "I've driven all the way from Exeter for this," he snaps.

"Like I said, I'm sorry." Ed's forehead ripples, the way sand goes when the tide's gone out. He looks *really* sorry. "The other person was so keen," he adds, "and I didn't have your number to call you. . ."

The man slams down the sticks and follows us downstairs. "Wasted journey," he complains as we see him out.

The fourth person asks if he can nip out for a smoke in our back garden. "To be honest," I hear him tell Ed, "I can't pay the prices you're asking. I'm, well . . . I'm a fan, you see. Couldn't resist coming round for a play."

Ed chuckles good-naturedly. I loiter at the open back door, ears pricked. "To be honest, mate, we've had a lot of those," he adds.

"Timewasters?" the man says.

"Nah. People like me and you. Genuine fans."

"Tell you what, though," the man says as I step out into our back garden, "*that's* what I'm looking for. Perfect size for my plot." He points at our rickety greenhouse with the smashed pots inside,

"That's funny," Ed says, "but you know what? We're selling it. Need the space. There's something else I want to build here."

"What?" I demand, whirling round to face Ed. "What are you building?"

Ed grins mischievously. "Little surprise."

"How much d'you want for it?" the man asks, grinding out his roll-up on our back step.

"Fifty quid should sort it," Ed says.

"But you can't sell it!" I cry. "It's . . . it's Dad's!"

Both men gawp at me. "Yeah, he can," Lily retorts, stomping back from Betty's garden. "It's horrible and spidery in there."

"But what would Dad say?" I hiss, realizing that Dad doesn't care about a scabby old greenhouse.

I watch Ed strut back into the house, then come out with a tape measure. Together, he and the stranger start measuring the greenhouse while the man scribbles on a scrap of paper. What's Ed planning to build in our garden anyway? A mini-gym? It's bad enough that he's dusted down Dad's old cycling machine and puffs and pants on it regularly. He'd probably use Cedric's wheel if he could squeeze himself into it.

The man leaves, returns shortly afterwards with a truck, and dismantles our greenhouse with Ed's help. There's no discussion with Mum – nothing. It's carted away bit by bit until all that's left are Dad's smashed tomato plants on the ground.

"That's fantastic," Mum gushes later. She's flushed with excitement after another day of selling holidays to places she's never been to.

"So I can start on the gym?" Ed asks.

So it *is* a gym, and we're all going to have to put up with Ed grunting and groaning in there. "Soon as you like, sweetheart," Mum says, grinning. And she kisses him on the lips.

Over the next few days, Ed's a whirl of activity. Despite the NO JOB TOO BIG OR TOO SMALL painted on his van, it's the first time I've seen him do anything that looks like proper work. First, a huge pile of rubble is delivered to form the gym's foundations. Then a friend of Ed's comes over and together they lay a concrete floor. It's Sunday evening when the phone rings. Mum says,

"Yes, there's one guitar left, and a bass and drum kit . . . half an hour? Yep, see you then."

I'm pretending to watch TV but it's all random pictures. My whole body slumps, as if someone's let all the air out of me. It'll be different this time. Ed's back at his own flat tonight, packing up the last of his things. He can't put the customer off with mad prices, or lie that someone's paid a deposit. It's just me and Mum, watching a cheesy game show, and Lily drumming upstairs.

The sunset guitar is propped on its stand next to the TV. Every time I imagined me and Riley in a band together, that was the guitar I'd be playing. Well, that won't happen now, with anybody. Because right now, someone is heading towards our house to take either that, the drum kit, or the battered old bass guitar away. They're the only things left.

Right now, I'd give anything for Ed to be here.

Shrivelling Up in the Bath

I'm lying in a warm, golden bath. It's golden because I've sloshed in loads of Mum's special moisturizing bubble bath, the stuff with real gold particles. If I lift out a hand, it's all shimmery, as if I'd cut up Jupe's leather trousers and made gloves out of them.

Mum would go mad if she knew. I don't care. She'll be able to buy hundreds of bottles of gold gloop from the money she's about to make.

I lie as still as I can, listening to the voices in the hallroom. That man's arrived, and his voice drifts upstairs.

Man: "I'm looking for something for my son. An electric, preferably, that he can really get stuck into. . ."

Mum: "Well, let's see, shall we? Come through and I'll show you. That's the bass, obviously. . ."

Man: "No, I'm not looking for a bass. . ."

Mum: "So how about this?"

A pause. I can picture this stranger picking up my

guitar, stroking its glass-smooth surface, thinking: *Yes, my boy would like this.* And I imagine Mum flashing her broad, open smile, the way she did to boost business at Tony's chippie, and the way she'll persuade people to book luxury holidays at the travel agents'.

Man: "This is nice, very nice. Quite special."

Mum: "Well, you know who owned it, don't you?"

Man: "Yeah." Pause. "Look . . . I have to be straight with you. I don't have a lot to spend. I just came round 'cause you're so local. You don't have anything more . . . ordinary, do you?"

Mum: " 'Fraid not. Why don't you try it anyway? There's a small crack here, d'you see? That's where it was mended but you'd never know, would you, unless you looked really closely. . ."

Man: "No, it's in really good nick. . ."

I poke my toes out of the water, expecting them to be gold too, like my hands. But the gold has gone, dissolved in the bath, like the pictures in my head of Riley and me in a band.

Mum: "Do you play?"

Man: "Not really. To be honest, I haven't picked up a guitar in years. . ."

Mum: "Go on, have a little strum. Or I could ask my daughter to play it for you – she's very good. . . I'll give her a shout, shall I?"

Man: "Doesn't she want to keep it?"

Mum (clears throat): "Um . . . I feel a bit bad about

this, actually. But we've been through quite an upheaval lately and, well . . . I'm thinking that, if I sell this stuff, I might be able to take my two girls on a proper holiday. . ."

What? She thinks I'd like a holiday more than Jupe's guitar? I want to jump out of this bath right now, fling on my dressing gown and rush down and tell her – but I can't, not in front of a stranger. I scowl at the toenails that I never get around to painting. What's the point, when you go to the beach to swim and mess about rather than posing in your bikini for the boys?

The man's finger-picking a song now. "It's a fantastic instrument," he says finally, "but I'm sorry, I'm not in your price league. . ."

"Look," Mum says, "take it away, see how your son gets on with it. Have it on loan for a while. Then maybe we can work something out. . ."

"Are you sure?"

No! I want to scream. *We're not sure at all. . .*

"I really want this to be over," Mum continues, "so we can all move on. It's not easy, you see, having my brother's things around. . ."

"Well, I can understand that," the man says, "and I'm sure my son would love it."

"Clover!" Lily hisses against the locked bathroom door. "There's a man downstairs! He's gonna—"

"Go away!" I hiss back at her.

"But. . ."

"Just leave me alone, go to bed." I glare at the film of gold scum that's now floating on the water and hear Lily padding across the landing to our room.

"Anyway," the stranger enthuses downstairs, "thanks so much for this, Mrs, er. . ."

"Kerry. Call me Kerry. . ."

"OK, um, Kerry, you know we'll take care of it. . ." There's more chatter which I can't pick up on my radar, then the front door clicks shut and he's gone.

I didn't even notice the bath water going cold, and now I'm shivering. The pads of my fingertips, which toughened up from a summer of playing, don't look like a guitarist's fingertips any more. They're just wrinkly from the water, like prunes.

40

Finding a Soulmate

Dear Jupe,

It's gone. The sunset guitar, I mean. I can't believe what Mum's done. I went downstairs and double-checked and yeah – she'd given it away.

Given it! "Why did you do it?" I yelled at her.

She looked totally shocked. "I thought we'd agreed. . ." she started.

"We didn't agree anything," I shouted back. Mum looked really sorry then, and tried to explain that the man had obviously been a big fan of Jupe's.

"I thought I was doing the right thing," she added, looking helpless. "He obviously loved your uncle's music. . ."

Obviously, it meant not a diddly thing that I loved you too.

Your niece,
Clover xxx

Over the next couple of days, I don't play much. I'm just not in the mood. Instead, I hang out in the garden with Ed, watching him building his gym. There's a proper concrete base now, and he's started to put up the brick walls. I can tell he's upset about the sunset guitar too, because he won't be drawn into talking about it – and anyway, he's too loyal to Mum. He's also way too busy to shout, "Hey, Clover! Play from the heart!"

Maybe I don't have the heart for music after all. I tell Jess about my plan to quit going to Niall's and take up – I don't know – the triangle instead.

"Don't be stupid," she retorts, lounging in shorts and a vest on my rumpled bed. "The triangle's not an instrument."

"What is it then?"

"It's . . . it's a *shape*."

"Well," I add, "I don't see the point any more."

"Is it because of Riley?" she asks. I pause, not wanting to admit that she's right, at least partly. "I can't believe you're thinking of stopping music because of him," she adds, "after your promise to Jupe and everything. . ."

"It's not that," I insist. "It's . . . other stuff."

Jess's cheeks flush. "Sorry," she mutters. "It's just. . . I think you should put him right out of your mind. . ."

"This is nothing to do with Riley Hart, OK? It's Jupe's guitar. Mum practically gave it away. . ."

"Well, aren't there any others left?" Jess asks, as if it's that simple.

"Just the bass," I grumble.

"Go fetch it, then," she commands.

"What for?" I ask, feeling dumber by the second.

"Let's have a play-about with it. If you're desperate for someone to play with, you can teach *me*."

"But I don't know how to play it either!" I say, exasperated.

"Of course you do. You've been learning guitar for long enough to play a little bit of bass, *and* you taught me those three chords. . ."

She only wants to help, so I can't tell her it'd be hopeless. "D'you still remember them?" I ask.

"What, A, C and G? Probably," she says with a grin. "Anyway, let's have a go."

The bass is languishing behind the TV, dulled by a thin layer of dust. Of course, Jess doesn't have a clue how to play it, and neither do I, but we plug it into the amp and work out which notes the strings are. She twangs experimentally while I try to play along on the acoustic. It sounds awful. I'm so glad Mum and Lily are out shopping with Ed, because he'd be up here in a second, bestowing us with his musical knowledge.

Then we start to sound a teensy bit less awful. I look at Jess, at her face all tanned from Majorca, scrunched in concentration. She's only playing two notes really, but they happen to be the right ones occasionally, and it no longer matters what we sound like because it's fun. "You should get some lessons from Niall," I tell her, knowing that her parents would think nothing of forking out for one-to-one lessons instead of group ones, like I have.

"Maybe," she says with a shrug.

"You can borrow this bass if you like."

"You sure?" she asks.

"Yeah, definitely."

We spend the next couple of hours playing and even manage to carry on when the others come back and Mum's music starts up downstairs. Lily comes up and picks out a rhythm on the drums, and we shut our bedroom door and keep on playing all afternoon. And it sets me thinking that maybe Jess is right – I really should put Riley right out of my mind. It's not as if I can't start a band without him.

As for Jess and Lily . . . well, we sound rough, of course, and I'd hate to think that Jupe is cringing at all our wrong notes and missed beats from his cloud. But doesn't everyone have to start somewhere?

Over the next week, Ed hammers and bashes late into the evening. "Nearly done," he calls out jovially when Betty peeps over the fence. She mumbles something I can't pick up. "Yeah, I reckon it'll be perfect," he adds.

"Mum," I venture, glancing through the kitchen window, "d'you mind Ed building a gym out there?"

"What?" she says. "Oh, that – um . . . well. . ." She shrugs. "To be honest, love, I was hoping Ed would give up all that bodybuilding stuff. He's such a softie, you know, underneath. . ." I shudder involuntarily. "Those muscles don't really suit him," she adds. Discussing Ed's body in any detail makes me feel pretty pukey, so I turn away and busy myself with drying the dishes. "Anyway," Mum adds, "was that Jess playing bass earlier today?"

"Yeah, she's just trying to find her way around it. . ."

Mum smiles. "You've been playing a lot this week. . ."

"It's not too noisy, is it?" I ask, expecting a lecture.

She pauses, then says, "It's not too bad, actually, and none of the neighbours have complained so far. In fact," she adds, "Betty told me she enjoys hearing young people's music. . ."

Right, so she needn't have sold the sunset guitar after all?

Mum's eyes sparkle. "Lily's pretty good, isn't she?"

"Yeah, a natural, I reckon."

"Thinking of starting a band, are you?" Mum asks.

A kernel of excitement fizzles inside me. "Yeah," I say firmly, "I think I am."

41

Dad Spills the Beans

Dad phones next morning, asking if I could pop round to his flat. I march round to his place and press the downstairs buzzer, even though the bottom door's unlocked. That way, if he's drawing Bernice in the nude, at least she'll have time to dive back into her clothes and be normal.

Dad comes down to greet me, all smiles. I needn't have worried about a nudie drawing scenario because Bernice isn't even here. "Listen," Dad says as we head up to the flat, "there's something I need to tell you."

"What is it?" I ask, loitering in the tiny kitchen while he makes tea. There's a photo of Dad and Bernice stuck to one of the cupboards on the wall. Their smiles look a bit frozen, as if they've asked a stranger to take the photo and it's taken too long.

"I, um. . ." He grins lopsidedly. "It's, ar. . ."

"Dad, what *is* it?"

He chuckles softly. "It's . . . you see, I wanted to clear

it with you first, and Lily of course, before . . . before I do anything. You're my number-one girls, you know that?"

I nod, and butterflies start up inside me. Guess I do know, even if I've felt a bit relegated lately.

"And . . . whatever happens," he stutters, "nothing's going to change that, OK?"

I nod. "Yeah, Dad."

"Clover, um . . . I might be getting married again."

The butterflies flit away and I'm all still inside. "But . . . aren't you still married to Mum?" I whisper.

"Yes, of course, but when that's all finalized. . ."

"When you're divorced, you mean?" My eyes fill with tears.

"Clover, sweetheart, it's not going to happen next week or anything, but eventually. . ." He holds me tight and I breathe deeply, wanting to stay there, being held by him. "You do understand, don't you?"

I nod and pull away. "It's all right, Dad. I mean, Mum's with Ed now. . ."

"It's all happened a bit quickly, hasn't it?"

"Just a bit," I say with a small laugh. We head out for a walk then, along the shore. Dad chats away but I'm not in the mood for talking.

"Clover," he says, turning to inspect my face, "is something else bothering you?"

I sigh, not wanting to go into the whole Riley thing with Dad. He wouldn't understand, and anyway, I'm banning myself from thinking about Riley these days. Instead, it's guitar stuff that spills out: about Mum giving away the sunset one, and how unfair it all is.

"That's not right," Dad agrees, sitting beside me on a rock. "Your mum shouldn't have done that. Not the special one. The one you—"

"Dad," I cut in, "I know Jupe was really upset when it broke, and there was a huge row and everything, but. . ."

He blows air through his nose. "You can say that again."

"What I can't understand is why we never went back to see him. It was an accident; I was only a kid . . . why didn't we ever get in touch with him again?"

It's Dad who goes quiet then. "Well . . . it was a pretty big scene," he begins.

"Yes, I know. . ."

". . .And it really shocked your mum, what she'd done, losing control of the car like that. . ."

"But we were all OK," I remind him. "The farmer helped us, and we took the train back home. . ."

"We might not have been, though," Dad says gently. "We missed a tree by this much." He holds his thumb and forefinger a centimetre apart.

"Did we? I don't remember that. . ."

"It's true, Clover. Your mum was in shock. She couldn't believe what she'd done. And all these years she's blamed Jupe for that. I know it sounds crazy, but maybe it was easier for her to direct all her anger at him instead of facing up to what could have happened. . ."

"*What* could've happened?" I ask.

Dad sighs, looking me right in the eye. "Well, we could've been injured or worse. . ."

I feel sick to my stomach. "Killed, you mean?"

"Who knows? We were very lucky."

I get up and start walking, my head spinning as I try to make sense of what Dad's said.

"That doesn't explain Jupe," I add as he falls into step with me. "Why didn't he ever want to see us again?"

"He did," Dad says, putting an arm around my shoulders. "He borrowed a car and drove to Copper Beach once, about a month after it'd happened. He came to our house, but your mum was at work, and he trailed around all the chippies in town until he found her."

"What happened then?" I ask, frowning.

Dad scrunches his brow. "They had a quick coffee together. As you can imagine, your mum wasn't particularly pleased to see him, and when she blurted out that she'd nearly crashed the car, Jupe was furious. He couldn't believe she'd put you and Lily in danger. He started shouting at her, right there in the café – Tony had to march him out."

"God," I breathe. "So he did care about us after all." I pause, thinking about all the times I wrote to him when he never replied. "I used to send Jupe letters, did you know that?" I add. "And he never wrote back."

"He tried to," Dad says hesitantly. "No, I didn't know you'd written, but I know he wrote to you."

"He didn't, Dad!" I protest. "It's as if he just stopped caring. . ."

Dad takes my hand and squeezes it. "He wrote to you," he says softly, "but your mum took the letters before you saw them."

"What – she hid them from me? Why?" My heart's beating hard and fast.

"I don't know, Clover. She probably threw them away. . ."

"But that's so unfair!" I cry.

We stop at the point where the stone steps lead up to the seafront. "If you were feeling bad about something – really bad, I mean – then you wouldn't want anything to remind you about it, would you?"

"But it was only letters," I snap. "How many were there, anyway?"

Dad shakes his head sadly. "Not many. Three or four, maybe. The thing is, we all make mistakes, we all do bad things we're ashamed of. . ."

I wonder if he's thinking about how he walked out on me, Lily and Mum. "But we don't lie, Dad," I say firmly.

"I think," he says, "your mum knew how much Jupe meant to you, and that if you'd seen his letters, that would have made you want to go back to Crickle Cottage even more. And she just couldn't do that.

Sometimes," he adds, holding my hand tightly, "it's easier to just let things fade away."

I fall silent as we head into town, trying to take it all in. Aren't adults incredible, the way they can just rub someone out, like a stain, as if they'd never existed? Lily might practise her cartwheels in our bedroom while I'm knee-deep in homework, and babble away when I'm trying to get to sleep – and sometimes, admittedly, I fantasize about Ed's mysterious shed actually being a new bedroom for me. A Lily-free zone with a shrieking alarm that'd go off if anyone under the age of thirteen tried to enter. But I can't ever imagine cutting her out of my life.

"I, um, I'd better get back," I say finally as we reach the end of the precinct.

"I'll walk home with you," Dad says.

"No, Dad, I'll be fine."

Dad nods. "OK. Um, Clover," he adds, "d'you mind not telling Lily about me getting married again? And don't mention it to Bernice, either, when you see her. . ."

"Why not?" I ask.

He smiles sheepishly. "I, um . . . haven't asked her yet," he says.

I plan to walk home the long way because I need time to think without Ed hammering away, making my brain judder. What's Mum going to say when I tell her I know about Jupe's letters? And why, when we hadn't been in touch all those years, did Jupe want us to sort out his stuff? Maybe he didn't have anyone else to ask. I can't imagine my life ever being that empty.

Instead of heading home – can't face Mum just yet – I decide to drop in on Niall and Jen instead. Baby Miles now greets me with a delighted grin. *Co-ba*, he calls me, which I think is his word for Clover. I take him in his buggy back to the seafront. He keeps shouting, "*Co-ba! Coba!*" to the seagulls, so I decide it means anything that makes him happy.

There's a big group of girls on the beach, shrieking while they dry off on towels and trying to wriggle out of bikinis without showing anything. There's a flash of blonde hair, and a familiar voice slices the breeze, but I keep marching on, pushing the buggy without looking back. There's so much buzzing around my brain now – Dad's wedding, Jupe's letters – that there simply isn't room for any Skelling in my head. Or Riley, for that matter. At least, most of the time. . .

By the time I've taken Miles home and arrived back at our street, all's quiet. There's no hammering or sawing. Maybe Ed's having a tea break, or had to go off and do a proper job.

It's so quiet, in fact, that I realize I can hear the thudding of my heart.

Riley is standing in front of our house, and he's

holding a guitar case. It's an old, faded case with fraying handles. And I know, even from here, across the street, what's inside it.

He sees me and nods coolly. I try to nod back, but the grin surges like a wave across my face.

Riley is clutching my sunset guitar.

Acting Cool

"Hi," comes my iciest voice. Riley looks especially cute today, but let's not dwell on that. Even more tanned now, which brings out the honeyed flecks in his eyes.

"I, um, need to talk to you," he says hesitantly.

Don't melt. Don't fixate on his gorgeous face. "Is this what I think it is?" I indicate the guitar.

"Yeah," he mutters to his feet.

Ah, one-word territory. "Did . . . my mum give it to your dad?" I ask.

"Uh-huh." He looks almost guilty. "Dad didn't realize it was yours," he adds. "He couldn't believe it was Jupe's, either, with your mum virtually giving it away like that. . ."

"I couldn't believe it either," I say dryly.

"So why, when she could've made a fortune. . ."

I shrug, forgetting that I'm supposed to be aloof. "You know what?" I say. "We've just spent a week at

Jupe's old place. I think Mum'd had enough. . ." Of course she had. That's why she didn't want to keep it. She wanted it out of her life, in the same way that she didn't want Jupe writing letters to me. "Anyway," I add, "how did you figure out it was mine?"

"I just started playing it – or *trying* to play it. . ." A smile flits across his lips, twisting my heart as if we're connected. "I looked through the pockets in the case," he continues, "to see if there was a chord book or some old songbook. Anything that'd help me. . ." He nudges a weed with his trainer. "Look, can I come in for a minute? There's something I want to show you."

I know I should grab my guitar and say I'm busy, which is what any girl with a smidge of self-respect would do. Instead I let him in, sensing my iciness melting away. He props the guitar against our kitchen table. Mum's left a note: *Gone swimming with Lily love Mum xx*.

Riley fishes out a scrap of paper from his jeans pocket. "This was in the guitar case. I think you should read it."

Frowning, I uncrumple it as best as I can and read:

Dear Clover,
I sincerely hope it's you who's holding this note. If it's not, and the finder – whoever you are – doesn't know a certain Clover Jones, then there's nothing for it but to screw up this letter and do whatever you will

with this guitar of mine. It no longer matters to me.

However, if it is you, Clover, then I want you to know that this guitar is for you. I don't care what happens to the rest of my stuff, and have left instructions for your mum to deal with it as she sees fit. But this guitar – well, it's very special to me, even though it caused me to lose my family and never see you again. Do you remember what happened?

You were nine or ten (you must be a teenager by now. That would make me feel really old, if I wasn't dead already). Your mum had warned me that I shouldn't let you play this guitar, but I insisted that you couldn't possibly damage it. I wanted you to find out for yourself what it could do. The way I see it, the instruments you play as a child should be special. That way, music imprints itself on your ears and your heart and stays with you for life. It changes you – for ever.

This guitar is special, Clover, more than you or your mum realized. It's a 1960s Fender, which means nothing unless you're a sad old dead muso like me. The guy who first inspired me to start playing gave it to me. It's pretty valuable. But this isn't about money. When you dropped it, I wasn't angry because of its value, but because your mum had warned me not to let you play it. You know what? All I heard, when I was growing up, was how clever and sorted my little sister Kerry was, and that I was just an aimless drifter with my music and crazy ideas. I should have listened to her, shouldn't I?

So I blamed you, Clover. I said you were selfish and stupid. I'll never forget how your face, which had been alive with excitement as you played, just crumpled. I knew there was no going back.

So you all left, and I'd lost my family.

I glance up at Riley. He's gone blurry as if I'm seeing him through a sliver of seaglass I've found on the beach.

I heard about the car accident, when I went to visit your mum when you and Lily were at school. Things didn't work out that day. I've never been very good at keeping my temper in check when it comes to things – or people – I care deeply about. But it's not surprising that your mum never got in touch with me again, not when I behaved so badly in front of her boss. . . Then, when I'd almost given up, I started to receive letters from you. I'm not the best letter writer and I've never had email – stuck in a time warp, aren't I? Anyway, from what you wrote, I don't think you were getting my replies. So I stopped after that. Still sent birthday cards, though. I hope you got them.

When I started to get ill with cancer, Clover, I had some decisions to make. The main thing was to find a good home for this guitar, so I want you to have it. As you can see, it was repaired and is virtually as good as new. My only request is that you don't smash it up on stage when you're a hugely famous rock star like your mad old uncle, haha.

With much love,
Jupe xxx

P.S. I know things are getting worse and I'll probably have to go to hospital soon. I have tried to rehome Fuzz with various neighbours in the village but he keeps sneaking back to Crickle Cottage, the batty old thing. Maybe you found him. Or maybe he found you.

"So . . . what now?" I say in a whisper.

"About what?" Riley's eyes are piercing mine.

"About the guitar. I can't keep it, can I? It's yours now. Mum gave it to your dad. . ."

"Are you crazy?" Riley exclaims. "You really think I'd keep it?"

"Well, er. . ." I mumble.

"God, Clover," he retorts. "You know what my dad's like. Believes in karma and all that, insisted I brought it straight back to you, said it's where it belongs. . ."

I nod. "Riley," I say hesitantly, "what happened this summer?"

He bites his lip. "You mean that time with Sophie?"

"Yeah. That time I came round to your place when Ske . . . when *Sophie* was there. It was her, wasn't it, who told you I'd said all that horrible stuff?"

Riley shrugs, and his ears turn pink.

"And you believed her," I add.

His eyes meet mine, sending a shoal of tiny fish darting around my stomach. "Yeah, at the time, I did. I know it was stupid. . ."

I fix on those hazel eyes, challenging him to believe her over me. "I'd never have said anything like that," I add.

His face clouds, and he looks around our kitchen as if not knowing what to do next. "I didn't know what to think," he adds. "You see, me and Sophie go way back. . ."

"You told me that already," I remind him.

"And . . . I know she can be a bit mean to you, but. . ."

"A *bit* mean?" I splutter.

"But she's not really like that," he adds, perching on the edge of our table. "Yeah, I know she seems really confident and full of herself, but there's other stuff you don't know about."

I stare at Riley. "What other stuff?"

He inhales deeply and looks at me, sending shivers right through me. "I'm sorry, Clover. I can't tell you. I promised I never would."

"But, Riley. . ."

"It's too important," he cuts in. "Then this happened – Dad bringing home your guitar and everything, and when I read the note . . . it was like a sign, you know? That I should come and see you and try to sort things out. I've, um. . ." He lowers his gaze. "I've missed you."

"But, Riley. . ." I pause. "I never know where I am with you. One minute we're . . . friends . . . the next, you're cutting me off, just like that. . ."

"I'm sorry," he mutters. "Now I guess I've really messed up."

"No, you haven't," I say quietly. "Maybe I did. It's been a weird time for me too."

We stand there for a moment, and I pray that Mum and Lily won't burst in. What happens next takes my breath away, as Riley steps towards me and wraps me up in his arms. "I wanted to come and see you," he says gently. "Jupe's letter kind of gave me an excuse."

I can't help smiling at that. *Thanks, Jupe*, I say silently.

"Hey," Riley adds, "maybe I was stupid to believe what Sophie said. She admitted, eventually, that she hadn't actually *heard* you saying that stuff about me, that it was just going around. . ."

"So you know she was lying?"

Riley nods. "I shouldn't have listened, but I guess I was just feeling touchy about the whole guitar thing. I know I'm rubbish, but I couldn't give up playing, could I?"

"Why not?" I ask, totally baffled now.

"Because. . ." he laughs, "if I stopped coming to Niall's and gave up guitar, I'd have had no excuse to be with you, would I?"

Isn't that the maddest thing? That Riley thought he needed an *excuse* to hang out with me? Something squeaks in the utility room, and we flinch and jump apart. It's Cedric, running on his wheel. You might think small rodents aren't good for much apart from scampering up people's sleeves, but let me tell you, they're brilliant at dispelling tension when you don't know what to say next.

By the time Mum and Lily come home, me and Riley are lounging and talking in my room. They're baking together downstairs. Mum seems to have a lot more time for us these days, and you know what? There's been another turning point. Her offerings used to often end up in the bin. The one time she produced fairy cakes for Lily's school spring fair, I spotted one of the other mothers quietly dropping them into a plastic carrier bag and putting them under the table out of sight. I felt so crushed when I saw that.

Anyway, the heart-shaped cookie was a definite improvement, and the chocolate brownie smells that are wafting upstairs are delicious too. In fact, our house smells even better than Jess's place.

As for my afternoon, that's pretty heavenly too. I play

the sunset guitar, and Riley sings. He's reluctant at first, saying his voice is rubbish and he doesn't know the words to any songs. So I grab a pen and paper and write out the words to that song – the one Jupe wrote for me. He never got round to thinking of a proper title so it ended up just being called "Clover's Song".

That's what we play. When Riley sings my name, it makes the back of my neck tingle as if Cedric's just scampered across it. I sort of wish Jess was here to add bass, because she's already sounding pretty good after one lesson with Niall and a few sessions here with me.

But really, I'm glad no one else is here in my room right now, or it wouldn't be just Riley and me.

43

The Band

New term starts, and the parched afternoons seem to stretch for ever. I haven't seen Skelling for ages and she'd slowly started to fade from my mind. In fact, I couldn't believe I'd been so wound up about her. First day back, though, I spot her heading across the playing field towards me at break. Unusually, she's on her own. No Amy or any of the other sidekicks.

"Good summer?" she asks.

"Er, yeah," I tell her. And something's changed. Maybe it's Skelling – she's not quite so cocky – or perhaps it's me, and she just doesn't faze me any more. "How about you?" I ask, because I feel like I should.

"It was all right," she says coolly. "Um, I hear you and Riley have been doing a music thing. . ."

I nod, waiting for the scathing remark.

"Seeing a lot of him, aren't you?"

"Yes, I am," I say firmly.

"It's just. . ." She flushes and looks away. "Me and

Riley have been friends since we were little, you know?"

"Yes, he told me that."

"And. . ." She pushes back her hair, which has turned even blonder during the summer. "He knows things about me that no one else does."

I stare at her. "Well, he hasn't told me anything, apart from the two of you knowing each other in Haven."

"Honestly?" For a moment, it's not Skelling any more. It's a scared girl who wants to believe I'm telling the truth.

"Honestly," I reply.

"You mean . . . he didn't tell you about my dad?"

I shake my head. Across the field, I see a small group of her mates laughing loudly, stealing someone's schoolbag and flinging it on to the parched grass. "He hasn't said anything, Sophie."

She peers at me, as if trying to decide whether I'm trustworthy or not. "Oh, you might as well know," she says sharply, the old, brittle tone creeping back into her voice. "My dad's been in prison, yeah? Got into trouble in Haven where we used to live. That's why we moved. Mum wanted to get away from everything. Then Riley and his dad moved here too, and she was petrified it was all going to come out. . ."

"But I'd never have thought. . ." I cut in.

"Course you didn't," she scoffs, jutting out her chin. "No one would. They all think I've got everything, right? But Riley knows I haven't. He knows my dad's been in trouble, and that we had to move 'cause so many people were waiting for him to come out of jail. . ."

"Is he out now?" I ask. "You said he had a new company car. . ."

She bursts out laughing. "It's not that kind of company car," she scoffs. "My dad's loaded, right, but he doesn't work for a *company*. . ."

"Oh." I try not to look dumbstruck.

"Yeah, he's out now but not living with us. Mum doesn't want anything to do with him. Listen. . ." Her face darkens. "You're not going to spread this around, are you? Mum would go mad if it gets out. . ."

"Of course I won't," I say quickly. "And honestly, Riley didn't tell me a thing."

She nods and turns away, heading towards her friends. "Well, good luck with your music thing."

"Thanks," I say, but I'm not sure she heard.

I don't mention Skelling's secret to Riley because it's between him and her and not me. And even though I've angsted over what's going on between them, I sort of like the fact that he kept it all to himself. It means he's trustworthy. I can't imagine many people knowing something like that and not blabbing. Anyway, now we're back at school, I don't have time to worry any more. With the "music thing", as she put it, we need all the time we can get.

By "we", I mean the band. That's right: *a real band.* Well, sort of. We're a bit like Dad's wonky back porch because most of the time it feels like we might fall to pieces at any moment. But somehow, by a whisper, we hold it together.

Our band doesn't have a name yet, because you hear about people debating for months – even years – what to call themselves, then they realize their time's run out and they've forgotten to write any songs. So, for the moment, we're just "us". That's (imagine me introducing them on stage, a spotlight falling on each band member in turn):

Riley Hart! (vocals)

Jess Williams! (bass)

Lily Jones! (drums)

And finally me, Clover Jones! (rhythm guitar)

At first I couldn't figure out where we'd practise. Mum's not averse to loud music but she *is* paranoid about upsetting the neighbours, and I knew she'd object to all four of us crammed into our bedroom. Then I found out that Ed wasn't building a gym after all, because he let slip that he was soundproofing the walls. It's a rehearsal room, in the back garden, where Dad's greenhouse used to be. He'd sworn Mum to secrecy. Ed said, "Just wanted to keep Jupe's memory alive. Isn't it right that there's live music around here?" Then he scurried away, all bashful, and put on Sky Sports really loud.

I know, though, that he's done this for Lily and me. Every so often he pokes his head round the door and says, "Is that *it*? That's as loud as you kids can play? When are you gonna let me join in?" Apart from that, it's perfect. I guess that, for Ed, this project wasn't too big or too small.

It's only Dad who's iffy about the whole band thing. Last time I saw him he said, "You're looking pale, sweetheart. Have you been spending all your spare time in that shed?"

I told him yes, and that it's not a shed but a *rehearsal room.*

"What a waste of the sun," he muttered. I know he's proud, though, because he's asked us to play at his wedding next year. "No pressure or anything," he said with a wink.

Maybe we will sound like a real band by then. Riley's voice is strong and pulls you right into a song. We all sort of work together: Jess is the beauty, Lily's our novelty for being so young yet bashing the hell out of her kit, and Riley's our token boy who'll get all the attention from girls. And me? Well, I guess I'm just me. I'm just ordinary Clover.

"I'd better head home," Jess says finally. "Mum'll go mad if I'm late on a school night."

I've lost track of time. Through the tiny window, the evening sky is streaked with purple. "Ugh, school," Lily huffs. "I'm going to see Fuzz." My sister adores that cat. I've tried to get on his good side and coax him over with leftover tinned tuna I found in our fridge, but he stalked off in disgust.

I hear Lily calling him, and her squeal of delight when he runs to her.

Now it's just Riley and me. He looks tired, and his voice is hoarse from hours of singing. "Shall we run through that last song again?" I suggest.

He shakes his head. "Sorry, I'm all done."

"So . . . what d'you want to do now?" I'm still shy around him when the others aren't here. When will I ever act like a proper thirteen-year-old?

Grinning, he comes over and takes off my guitar, zipping it into its faded case. He touches my face, starting those tiny fish up again. His kiss is light as a feather on my lips.

"This," Riley says. "Let's do this."

44

Dear Jupe

Dear Jupe,
It's over a year since you died. I can hardly believe it. I wanted to say thank you for the guitar and for forgiving me for breaking it.

I also wanted to tell you I play it all the time, and Lily's doing great stuff with your drums. We're playing at Dad and Bernice's wedding in a couple of months, which we're all excited about. Who knows – maybe we'll play at Mum and Ed's one day too. Of course Ed will insist that we're very, very loud and to play from the heart and all that!

I should mention she and Dad split up (it all seems a long time ago now). Mum's in love with a man called Ed, who's a huge fan of yours. D'you know, he once paid hundreds of pounds for an old handwritten songbook of yours? He showed it to me recently. It had the lyrics and chords for "Clover's Song" in it – the one you wrote for me! I'd never seen it written down before. I didn't even know you had a book like that. The first time Ed played it, I nearly fainted with shock because I couldn't understand when he could have possibly heard it. It was almost as if you were in the room, controlling his voice and fingers.

Now, of course, I know he just learnt it from your little book. He still plays it sometimes. Well, murders it, really. But he's OK. In fact, we're all more than OK. I feel a lot better knowing you did write back to me. When I confronted Mum about your letters, she said she hadn't wanted me to read anything scary or angry from you. She didn't want me to have those memories. She still cared about you, though, because she'd never been able to bring herself to throw them away. She showed me where she'd hidden them – in a little wooden box on the shelf in the porch where we keep Cedric's food. I'd almost touched them, Jupe! And they weren't angry at all. They were friendly and chatty (at least, I think they were – have to say your writing's terrible).

As for Lily, she's looking very grown up. Keeps nagging me to put her hair in an updo the way Bernice did once. She had to make a collage of our family for her Brownie art badge and it's taken her for ever because she couldn't figure out who should be in it. Of course she put me, Mum and Cedric in it. Then she decided you should be there, and Dad –

and if Dad was in it, then Bernice should be too, and Ed . . . plus Fuzz was a last-minute addition. So we're all there, and it's pretty crowded, so I guess she's fine about the new shape of things.

So now Ed's living here and your songs fill our house all the time. When you died I made a promise that I'd get a band together and make it one day. Now I think I was really promising myself. And we're getting there. We're going to make it.

D'you know that, Jupe? I think you do. Every time I play it's like you're here with us again.

Love,
Clover xxx

P.S. I have your gold leather trousers. Haven't dared to wear them yet.
P.P.S. You'll be pleased to hear that Fuzz, who now lives with Betty next door, is the most pampered cat in Copper Beach.

Acknowledgements

Huge thanks to my super-agent, Caroline Sheldon, and to Clare Argar, Alice Swan, Polly Nolan and all at Scholastic for bringing this book to life. Further back, this idea formed when my friends Kevin and Fliss formed a band (hello Teignmouth!) so thanks for such great times. I'd be lost without my writing group, especially Tania, Vicky, Amanda and Margaret, and my lovely friends Cathy, Jenny, Kath, Riggsy and Wendy V. Big thanks also to former avid-teen readers Hannah Currie and Becky Varley-Winter (who nudged me in the right direction all those years ago) and to Sam, Dex and Erin for tons of ideas. Above all, thanks to Jimmy, for helping this story to form and for putting up with me tapping away late into the night.

Life Death and Gold Leather Trousers is your first book for teens – what were you like as a teenager?

I loved music, drawing, reading and writing stories and decided at around fourteen that I either wanted to work on a teenage magazine or be an illustrator. I started drawing little comic strips and sending them off to comics, and occasionally a cheque for all of £5 would arrive in the post, which seemed like SO much money. As an only child, I lived in my own imaginary world a lot – it was good training for being a writer. I wasn't really a fashion or make-uppy kind of girl until I reached about sixteen, when I became obsessed with the 1960s and started backcombing my hair, wearing ski pants and white lipstick and tons of black eyeliner. Until then, I'd just liked messing about on my bike, writing, or doing art.

In the book, Clover is very into her music – did you ever play an instrument or want to be in a band?

I played a bit of guitar and flute at school, then saxophone. I was in a couple of very short-lived bands in Dundee, playing in grimy pubs, when I first left home.

And who were your favourite band when you were a teenager?

I loved The Jam, Echo & the Bunnymen *and also sixties bands like* The Beatles, The Kinks *and* The Rolling Stones.

We never meet Jupe in the book, but he comes across as quite an eccentric character – is he based on anyone you know?

He's a mixture of various rock stars from the '70s, little bits from lots of different people.

What was the last CD/music download you bought?

I haven't bought music for ages as my family buys so much. Jimmy, my husband, bought Fleet Foxes *yesterday, which I love. I tend to listen to the radio while I'm writing – I hate writing in silence.*

Where is your favourite place to write?

In my tiny boxroom – it's warm, cosy and crammed with notebooks with Post-it notes stuck all over the place. I also like writing in cafés or on trains – I'd go mad, being stuck at home all the time.

Do you ever test out your stories and ideas on your friends and family?

My daughter Erin read parts of Gold Leather Trousers, *and a writer friend read the whole book at a very early stage, and gave me the confidence to polish it up and keep working on it.*

What tips would you give for young writers?

It's harder to write a story than to have an idea for a story – so it's vital to get the words down, even if you don't feel very confident or want to show your story to anyone at that stage. You can always work on it, improve it, go back to it weeks or months later. It usually gets better and better and eventually you know it's the best you can make it. That's when you should give it to people to read.

LDAGLT is absolutely hilarious, but it also has some really poignant moments – particularly between Clover and her parents. What inspires you to write in this way?

I wanted Clover and her family to feel real, and real people have all sorts of things happening to them – funny and sad. It was important to have funny parts as I absolutely didn't want this to be a gloomy book. I did think, though, that it needed some real drama and sadness to be a compelling story.

Which book (that has already been written) do you wish you could have written and why? Or are there any that you would like to rewrite?

I loved How I Live Now, *by Meg Rosoff, and* Ways to Live Forever *by Sally Nicholls – beautiful, touching books with unforgettable characters. One holiday in France, my three children and I all read* Ways to Live Forever, *with each person impatiently waiting for their turn. And I love Cathy Cassidy's books too –* Dizzy *is my favourite. My kids and I all read* The Curious Incident of the Dog in the Night-time *– absolutely brilliant. I read as much teen fiction as adult books.*

Tell us a strange fact about yourself.

I used to live on a narrowboat on the canal in North London.

Have you ever owned a pair of gold leather trousers?

No, in fact no leather trousers at all – too shiny. And jeans are better for walking my dog.